Walk With The Magician

C. S. Clifford

First published in Great Britain 2017

ISBN: 9 780993 195778

Printed and bound in the UK

A catalogue record of this book is available from the British Library

Edited by Chloe S Chapman

Cover by Anna E Howlett of Rosehart Studio

For the continued inspiration I receive from
the children I teach.

To Jack

Best Wishes

Prologue

Matt and James discovered a portal to another time and place at the start of their summer holidays, by chance, during their training to get fit for the approaching rugby season. While swimming underwater in the local river, Matt had found a cave at the base of a waterfall. The two boys eagerly explored the cavern and tunnel leading from it to a second waterfall. Running alongside was a narrow ledge which allowed them to pass through the deluge into a strange new world. This is their fourth adventure through the waterfall and into the unknown…

Chapter 1: Decision Time

James sat idly on the bank of the river, lost in a sense of peace. He watched the water slide gracefully past carrying an assortment of debris from the trees that reached over and deposited from the opposite side. The once living material had been savagely ripped from their anchors by the fierce and brutal wind that had lasted for the past few days.

"Do you realise that the first three weeks of our summer holidays have lasted over three months thanks to us visiting the past. I love the way that time stands still here when we go through the portal," he said in a reflective tone.

"I know, isn't it great? Three weeks ago we sat here thinking of ways to get ourselves fit for the coming rugby season and thanks to the adventures we've had,

I think I am almost at my peak fitness level. I feel stronger, faster and fitter than ever before," Matt replied.

Younger by almost a year and shorter by nearly a head, he was stocky in frame. At the age of fourteen he was already starting to broaden at the shoulder and taking on a muscular definition. He was proud of the way his physique was developing, knowing that it would make a real difference to his game.

"I'm thinking that it's about the time for us to go through the portal again," James stated emphatically.

"Well I never thought I would see the day when your enthusiasm for something beat mine," Matt teased his lifelong friend.

"Have you noticed the way your body is changing, or rather developing, I am sure you were a lot skinnier at the start of the holiday?"

James looked down at his own body. Slimmer, lighter and with longer legs, he was faster than his friend but just as strong. His more graceful limbs belied the strength his muscles contained.

"Care to put your body to the test against mine, maybe a series of challenges to suit everything we need for the rugby season?" James dared.

"Always up for a challenge you know that but, now that you've mentioned it, I think you're right, it is time we went back through the portal and had another adventure. When do you want to do it?"

"Tomorrow for sure, I'm getting restless and want to meet some new people, make some more friends, see a new landscape, and have a new adventure. You know, experience again all the things that happen to us when we go through."

Matt's eyes widened in excitement as he started to feel the tingle of anticipation that James was already experiencing. He broke into a huge grin.

"Tomorrow it is then, let's go early. Why don't we walk up stream a little towards the waterfall and see if our things are still where we left them?"

James already knew that their belongings, carefully hidden, would still be there but he felt the same as Matt. The need to go and see the place that hid the secret portal and enjoy the feeling, that they knew something that nobody else in the whole world did, was powerful. He was on his feet before he finished agreeing to the idea.

Twenty minutes later he and Matt stood before the waterfall and watched the water tumble into the river below. They saw it swirl and momentarily fight the current that headed downstream before it acquiesced.

They thought about the hidden secret that lay below the water, a secret that they had shared with nobody, and one they guarded as passionately as they did their own twenty-five yard line on the rugby pitch.

The rope that had once been tied to a tree and snaked down to the bottom of the waterfall had been removed. James had been concerned that somebody else might decide to swim down and discover their secret. They didn't need it anymore; they knew the twist and turns inside the underwater cave.

"You know we don't have to wait until tomorrow, we could go right now. With time standing still here when we go through, it doesn't make a difference to anybody except us," James said grinning.

"I have a dentist appointment tomorrow and I know I am going to have a filling," Matt responded.

"If we go through now you will still have the appointment tomorrow when we come back even if we spend a year in the next place."

"I don't think I want to spend that long in another place, the rugby season will never arrive at that rate.

Besides the tooth has been playing up a bit so I want it done"

"You're right of course, but come on, what the hec, let's just go now."

Matt stared at his friend with surprise wondering what was up with him as he was not displaying his normal reserved approach.

"What! I'm just feeling restless, and anyway can't I make the first move for once?" James responded to the quizzical look.

"Yes, I mean of course you can, we're a team."

"Well come on then," James said grinning broadly and suddenly dived into the water fully clothed.

He ducked under the surface and Matt laughed at this side of James' developing personality.

Before their previous adventure James hadn't ever been that impulsive. He was changing – had to be down to all their time travel. He waited for a moment just in case his friend was playing a trick on him but then after realising that James had been under the water too long to be coming back this way he dove in and swam down.

A few powerful strokes and Matt reached the opening of the underwater cave and swam right into it. It didn't remain horizontal for very long and started to angle upward and veer first to the right and then to the left. As the blackness engulfed him he made his way by touch noticing how much easier the underwater journey was now compared to the first time he had ventured in and almost ran out of breath. Above he noticed a shimmer of light that penetrated the blackened depths to his position and he knew he was almost there. As the light intensified his head broke the surface and he raised a hand to shield his eyes from the beam of a torch James pointed towards him.

"Took your time!" James said angling the torch away from Matt as he clambered up out of the water and sat alongside.

"Had to make sure you weren't playing a trick or something on me, this is hardly the way you normally act is it?"

"I can be impulsive like you sometimes, anyway if you have got your breath back, I think it's time to go and see where we are going to next."

"I'm not out of breath at all; I was just thinking how much easier the swim is these days."

"I know what you mean, I found it effortless too."

The two of them looked involuntarily around to see if anything had changed, nothing had, why would it, they only passed through here a few days ago?

"Come on, let's go," Matt said taking his customary lead back from his partner.

James grinned to himself, *normality restored.*

They head off down the tunnel that led from the pool they had just emerged from and moved towards an increasing volume of sound from ahead. Diffused light that shimmered on the walls announced they had come to the end of their journey as they faced a second waterfall.

"I'll go first," James said and took a step towards the falling torrent of water.

"What, and spoil the habits of a lifetime," Matt said almost running to the water's edge in an effort to take the lead.

Without another word he sidled towards the left of the waterfall and allowed his foot to search for a narrow ledge that ran through and beyond the water. He found it effortlessly and followed its path through the deluge with James right behind him. Both boys held their breath until they were through the water and stepping off the ledge onto a succession of rocks that led the way down to ground level.

"Wow, would you look at that view James, from here we can see for absolutely miles in all directions; where do you think we are?"

"Not exactly sure but the rolling hills and woodland suggest middle England somewhere. There is no sign of any agriculture going on and I can't see any signs of habitation so we must have gone back in time a considerable amount."

"Not as far back as the last time, the torrent in the waterfall wasn't as heavy," Matt replied referring to their previous trip through.

"Your right but it was heavier than the time we went back to Sherwood."

"So sometime between 0 and 1000 years ad."

"That's about as close as we are going to get without gaining some more clues."

James turned his body around taking the scene in for the complete 360 degrees and absorbing the hundreds of shades of green that stretched in every direction, He stared and stared before turning to Matt with a frustrated look on his face.

"What is it?" Matt asked noticing the look.

"The scenery stretches for miles in every direction and there doesn't seem to be a single break in it apart from the occasional river or stream. I can't make out any sign of a trail or path which means we will be travelling blind as far as direction goes. It also means we are going to be walking for hours before we are likely to find a village or something."

"What are you worried about, that just adds to the mystery of the place. I reckon you are right though, we are still somewhere in England, look at those trees, I can see oaks, chestnuts, and silver birch."

"They have them abroad too, on the continent; so in theory we could be somewhere like France but my gut instinct still says England."

"I'll go along with that too."

"So which direction do we take then Matt seeing as you like to take the lead on things like this?"

"Easy, let's follow that river down there, if we have gone back in time as far as we think then communities would exist where there's water, that's how London was formed, I learnt that in history."

Matt didn't wait for confirmation from James, he just set off. James fell in alongside him and they covered the first few miles in relative silence enjoying the experience of being alone in such a vast countryside.

The river twisted and turned meandering through the landscape, its course following the slightest depressions at its depths, and soon it turned towards a wooded area.

It wasn't a huge woodland site but it was densely populated with birch and hazel trees which made passing through it difficult and laboured. As far as they could see there wasn't even an animal trail to follow.

Soon the boys were perspiring profusely with the effort but neither stopped their forward motion for a rest from the toil. Then, without any visual warning, they emerged into the open once more.

Matt was about to continue when James placed his hand on his friends shoulder and raised a finger to his own lip in the sign for quiet. Matt responded immediately and closed his eyes to help his ears take the leading role of his senses. They soon attuned to the surroundings and he could hear distant birdsong that he hadn't noticed before and then something else, something rhythmic, something that didn't sound like it came from a creature of the country. The dull thudding continued and James pointed to his left indicating that it was coming from the edge of the woods a way off.

Carefully, and as quietly as he could, he moved forward following the direction of the sounds with Matt close behind. He took his time making sure that wherever he placed his feet there was nothing that he would tread on that would make a sound and give away his presence. The thudding increased as they closed in until it seemed to James that the sound came from right next to him. Still he could see nothing and then, a screech, a screech so loud that it sent a shiver through James and Matt's bodies and neither could prevent themselves from shaking with the fear and shock of it...

Chapter 2: What Was That?

The screech came again, louder this time, if that was possible, a screech that penetrated to the remotest reaches of the human soul and threatened to panic and spoil the peace and calm that normally resided there.

James risked a whisper as he cowered lower on the ground. “I have never heard anything like that in my whole life, what the hec is it?”

“I haven’t a clue but it doesn’t sound like something friendly or anything that wants to be bothered by us. I think we should get away from here, it is the sensible thing to do.”

Before they could stand and move away, the screech came for a third time, not quite as forceful as before, but no less intimidating.

“Could it be a bird do you think James?”

"That's not like any bird I've ever heard."

James started to stand when the sound of a human voice stopped his upward motion. The voice sounded frail, old, and yet had an air of authority about it.

"What is it Aragon, why are you making such a sound that shatters my ears and takes away the focus from my work?" The voice asked in not much more than a whisper.

Whatever Aragon was its next sound definitely wasn't human either. Deeper and softer, almost affectionate, a much more sombre version of the screech came and was repeated several times.

"Hush now my friend," the voice whispered.

"It's so close James I can almost feel it, and yet I cannot see it."

"I know, what does your instinct tell you to do now, walk away from it or go and confront it?"

"You know me, I'm up for anything, but everything so far tells me to be on my guard and get ready for the unexpected."

"Know what you mean; ok let's do it."

The two of them stood side by side, as they would on the rugby pitch, and took a few more steps towards the sounds and the voice. Neither made an attempt to prevent any sound their footsteps might make.

Around a slight bend, the edge of the woodland fell back into a natural recess. There, at the heart of it, stood a crude shelter made of branches forced into the ground in a semi-circular shape. The space between them was filled with clods of grass that still lived in its most unlikely position. The roof had been fashioned out of layers and layers of straw tied together like a modern day thatching, but in this case much more rudimentary.

An old man sat at the entrance to the small dwelling shaping wood with a crude knife and a small stone used to hammer along the back edge of it. It was this that had caused the first sound that had alerted the boys of the presence of another.

The man was dressed in a long robe that covered his entire body. The hood, at this moment, was pulled down exposing a tangled mess of long white hair half way down to the middle of the man's back. A full beard accompanied the front of his face tapering to a point at least twenty centimetres long.

At first he did not sense their presence but from behind him came another full bodied screech that threatened to raise the roof of the shelter. Both boys winced at the sound and involuntarily ducked again and this movement finally alerted the old man of their presence. As they rose their eyes met the strangers'.

Seeing them the old man stood up hopping from one leg to another in a sprightly manner that belied his advanced age.

"So you've come then, I have been expecting you but still you have arrived sooner than I thought. I trust you found this place readily enough?"

"The journey has been long but simple." James replied instantly taking on a role that seemed to fit the situation.

"We could have travelled past this place and missed it entirely if it wasn't for some awful sounds that came from here."

"When Aragon speaks the whole world hears, he is the last of his kind and as such is constantly in danger from those who hunt him."

"Who or what is Aragon?" Matt asked his curiosity getting the better of him.

"Have you never heard of Aragon, son of Dreyfus and Marthonius the greatest dragons ever to fly in the world of men?"

"No I haven't."

"Then let me call him to us so that you can gaze upon the creature for the first time. Aragon, come to me my friend."

A rustling sound came from the woods behind the dwelling and a creature, like nothing the boys had ever seen, emerged through the dense melee of saplings at the edge.

"Come Aragon, come and greet our friends so that we can complete the courtesy of formal introductions."

Aragon sauntered forward and took a position alongside the old man. It was approximately three metres in height but twice that in length, due to a very long and scaly tail. The boys couldn't tell the true width of the creature for its wings were folded backwards and held tight to the body. The neck however, was long and elegant and held one of the most frightening heads that either Matt or James had ever seen. Long and bony and the only part of the creature, apart from the claws on its feet, that was not covered in scales. The eyes were situated high and towards the back of the head and were located above the jaws of the creature. Extending sixty centimetres or more the jaws were terrifying. Jaws that, when opened, revealed a double row of evil looking incisors that were clearly used to rip its victims flesh from their bodies. Then at the end of the upper Jaw and just a few centimetres back were two large nostrils that appeared to be smoking slightly. Both boys breathed in deeply.

"It is truly an incredible creature, and it breathes fire?" James asked guessing the reason behind the smoke.

"Yes he is and, if he is allowed to, he will grow up to be larger and stronger than his father and will be a legend in his own right. And yes, he started fire breathing only a week ago and already he has directional control and can project it a fair distance."

"How old is it exactly?" Matt asked.

"He hatched only three weeks ago. I was there myself to witness it and as I was the only living thing near it, it adopted me as its parent."

Matt and James couldn't take their eyes of the creature and the once drab brown colour of its scales changed to iridescent blues and greens similar to the colours on a drake.

"You said you were expecting us and yet we had no idea that we were going to meet you," James said.

"That is sometimes the way of a man's destiny. Often he is the last one to have his path revealed to him and it is clear that this is the case with you two. But before I speak to you of such things let me ask you of the names you go by."

"Of course, how rude of me! I am James and my friend here is Matt."

"I am pleased to greet the both of you and welcome you to my humble abode. I am Merlin master magician and advisor to King Arthur, or at least I was until a recent development placed aspersions on my allegiance to him and I was forced to flee Camelot for here."

Matt couldn't help but draw in a deep breath of surprise, for the second time in a few minutes as he realised he was looking at a man that held as much mystery and intrigue as any man in history ever had.

"We are pleased to meet you and Aragon Merlin; you honour us by inviting us to your hearth."

James smiled recognising the subtle change in the way Matt had spoken. Already they were adapting to the characters they were portraying to Merlin.

He immediately wondered what he now looked like. Only Matt would be able to see him as James and this happened every time they came through the portal. The only way they could see what they looked like in this world was to see their reflection in water.

Merlin interrupted his thoughts by inviting them to share some refreshment with him to which they both accepted.

The boys sat down opposite Merlin only too aware that Aragon had not diverted his eyes away from them. The old man reached for his staff which leant against the side of the dwelling and shook it and said a few words that neither Matt nor James could understand. There was a small puff of smoke and a platter of meat appeared before them along with horns used for drinking vessels.

"Wow! That's a neat trick, I wonder if we could learn to do such things?" Matt said in surprise.

Merlin indicated to the platter and James took a slice of meat. It looked like pork and it tasted like pork, juicy and succulent.

"This is good," James complimented

"Take what you will, there is always plenty where that came from, just offer the odd slice or two to Aragon. He is yet to master the subtleties of table manners."

James nodded and passed a piece to the dragon. The creature was incredibly quick and took the piece from James' out-stretched hand before he could register what had happened. He pulled his hand back to check that all his fingers were still intact.

The boys tucked in happily and held a horn up for Merlin to pour some fresh water from a bucket to one side of him. He didn't eat himself though and was content to watch the boys.

"You will rest a while and recover from your journey here and then I will tell you of the purpose of your visit and the quest that awaits you," The old man told them.

Both Matt and James immediately felt sleepy and they decided to lay back and shut their eyes.

"There is nothing like the powers of persuasion and a little magic here and there is there Aragon? I hope there is more to these two than what is apparent for their journey ahead is fraught with perils that will appear with regularity. And then to confront the one who has tarnished my name and reputation? Mmm! There are few in the world today with the presence and iron of mind and heart that could accomplish the task and, to be honest my friend, I have my doubts that they will succeed."

Merlin looked hard at their faces.

"Rest well my friends for you will need every ounce of your strength and resolve," he said and went back to the task he was tending too when the boys first heard him.

Chapter 3: The Quest

The boys awoke an hour later feeling as refreshed as ever they could. James sat up and found himself looking straight into the eyes of Aragon. He shuddered involuntarily and cursed himself for the shiver of fear that journeyed down his spine. He held the stare determined to rid the feeling and told himself it was just like lining up against an opponent that was twice his size. Matt stood up and the creatures gaze turned towards him.

"Wow! I feel so good after that nap. I don't often kip in the afternoons but I must have needed it."

James didn't answer back but he knew how his friend felt because he was feeling as good himself. His mind was now focussed on what Merlin had told them before they slept. That they would be told about the quest that they had been summoned here for; Merlin appeared from inside his dwelling.

"I thought I heard you stirring. My guess is that you can't wait to hear about your quest so I won't delay you for too long. Sit, make yourselves comfortable, have some more food or water if you wish."

The boys did as they were invited and waited for Merlin to perch beside them...

"It all started about three cycles of the moon ago. The land was riddled by a cruel disease that spread without prejudice between rich and poor, man and woman.

I said it was cruel because everybody fell victim to it but it only took one member of each family to the grave. That is of course, apart from the occasional second who was already sick with something else.

I don't believe there is a family in the country that didn't lose someone. The King was no exception either.

"I was living at Camelot at the time working on some magic to place on the crops the people have been sowing. We've had four consecutive bad harvests and the poor, particularly, have suffered because of it.

Anyway when the disease struck and the people went sick and the King commanded me to find a way to cure them but despite my best efforts I could not. This told me something about the disease, it wasn't natural and was probably caused by a spell, a spell from a Witch. There are several around here with the power but only two that I know of who are evil enough to cast it. Even then there must have been something to encourage the Witch to do it, a huge payment or something else that she wanted.

"I had to face the King to tell him that I had failed just after he lost one of his sons.

"The death had changed him, made him angry, as the grief of the loss took its toll. The decisions he made became wild, careless, call it what you like and he banished me from the castle.

"I should stress here that King Arthur is a good man, a kind man and a very compassionate King to his people. He has maintained a peace in the country for the longest period that anybody can remember, but he was not himself and even the lovely Queen could not get him out of his state of mind.

"About one cycle of the moon ago I received word that the King wanted to see me. It was about the time when the disease had finished and all had recovered from the torture of it. I travelled to Camelot and knelt before him. I asked him to forgive the frailties and inadequacies of his ageing magician but he wouldn't grant me the peace I was seeking. Instead he told me of another problem that he sought my help with."

Merlin was a talented narrator and the boys had neither chewed on the piece of meat that they held in their fingers nor drank from their horns. Instead both were captured in the moment of the story and didn't flinch as Merlin quenched his thirst.

"At some time during the height of the sickness Excalibur had been stolen from the castle. Now you may well ask why that is so important because it is only a sword but I am sure that you know the legend behind it, about how King Arthur withdrew it from a rock when no other man could and about how he wielded it in battle and brought peace to the land.

"Let me tell you that the sword has as much symbolic meaning as the round table King Arthur uses to show that all men are equal. The sword is important, it makes Arthur seem invincible, prevents others from possibly attacking him.

"I promised him that I would do all I could but he warned me that if I failed I would never be allowed to set foot in Camelot or be granted an audience with him again.

"Of course, the King was still grieving his loss but I have never known him to go back on his word.

"I have used all the magic at my disposal to try and discover where the sword was taken to, but to no avail. I searched the countryside and investigated the crime in the way of men by seeking out every known informer and offering money for information as to the swords whereabouts. I hoped to discover the identity of the thief but received no clues until a week ago when I stumbled upon a merchant, an honest, hardworking man who sought no reward for the information he gave me.

"The merchant was in Camelot, toward the end of the sickness period, to restock on supplies for the road.

"His departure from the castle had been delayed as he had visited with an old friend. Instead of waiting until the following morning, he decided to leave late in the evening after sharing a final meal. His reason for leaving so late was simple, he preferred to sleep under the stars than in the confines of a castle walls.

"He had been travelling for about an hour and was close to the spot where he would camp for the night when he was overtaken by a group of men in full armour and on horseback. He took no real notice of them as they passed by for it was a particularly dark night with no moon. He gave them no more thought until he chanced on me.

"With careful questioning he remembered more than he thought he would and could describe the coat of arms that decorated the men's shields; Sir Thomayne.

"Sir Thomayne was a knight of the round table but was not particularly favoured or trusted by many. I know from overheard conversations that some had a notion to get him removed from the table but proof of any wrong doing had not been uncovered.

"His coat of arms portrays a bear jumping over two cross swords and there are no others that resemble this. The merchant remembers that the men were riding hard and in afterthought was surprised because that can be fraught with potential danger from unseen obstacles, especially on a night like the one he described.

"At the time of the swords disappearance Sir Thomayne was the only knight present at the castle who left. The others stayed there and those that were not there were away on the King's business. Not exactly any proof of Thomayne's involvement I know, but the truth is only one of the knights could have got anywhere near the sword and, since the castle and the ground within its walls have been thoroughly searched, he is the only one with the opportunity to have got it out."

"What do we know about Sir Thomayne's current whereabouts?" James asked.

"Little and nothing really! The merchant said he was heading west and there is little in that direction between Camelot and the Northern Sea; I can only think of two small villages."

"Did you travel there to investigate further?"

"I wanted too but my magic failed me. As you can see for yourselves I am not the youngest in these parts nor am I the fittest and I do not possess a horse.

"Normally, my magic takes me from one place to another but it will only take me a few miles west of Camelot. There is nothing wrong with my magic in any other direction, I can travel for as far as I desire which tells me of something else. To the west lies a barrier, an unseen barrier, but one that prevents my magic working. There can be only one reason for this and my thoughts suggest that it has been placed there by a Witch. I believe that it is the same one who brought the sickness upon us. This also tells us that she has conspired with somebody rich and powerful and it is my opinion that it is Sir Thomayne."

"So from what you tell us so far it is my guess that you want James and I to travel west, find the location of Sir Thomayne, retrieve the sword and return to Camelot with both, oh, and thwart a very powerful Witch in the process."

"You have understood the task well Matt but you will not be completely alone for you are to take Aragon with you. I will not be able to travel the full distance because the Witch will sense my powers even if I cannot use them. However, she will not foresee the arrival of Aragon because there is nothing magical about him. He is a creature pure and simple.

"Aragon does possess a connection of the mind with me. We can communicate from great distance and I can see what he sees. There is risk to his accompanying you for there will be those who would try to kill him and seek the rewards, which dragon slayers throughout history, have sought; lands and titles. It is a powerful incentive especially if you are poor."

"You being able to communicate with Aragon isn't exactly going to help us if you are not with us to translate what he sees."

"You are correct James and because of this I have mixed you a concoction that will allow you to communicate with Aragon as well. Although you cannot speak directly with me you will be able to hear my thoughts and plans if you go through Aragon."

"We don't have much experience of looking after dragons," Matt stated.

"You do not need to for Aragon is completely self-sufficient. Although he will travel with you, he will not actually be with you. If you like think of him as an invisible guardian, he will be there but just not visible."

"How does that work, you said he didn't have magical powers?"

"He doesn't. He must not travel in the same direct route as you for fear of being seen. His journey will take place at night, but even if you travelled all day and he remained here, he would still be able to see you.

"Slightly north of your westerly travel and on the cliff tops at the edge of the Northern Sea is an old castle. Most of it was in ruin a decade ago and nobody, to my knowledge, has inhabited the place since. It would be an ideal place to use to hide in, if that is, you were not afraid of the curse that was placed upon it at the death of its previous owner."

"What curse? James asked.

"It is better that you don't ask that question for if you don't know it, it cannot affect you."

"When do you want us to leave?"

"That question tells me that you have accepted the quest. It is such a relief that the burden is now shared. We will leave together as soon as I have gathered a few things to take with me."

"What about a horse for you to ride Merlin?" James asked worried about the old man's frailty.

"We will all use horses for the first part of the journey but mine will disappear when we reach the invisible barrier."

Merlin waved his staff and said a few unknown words and three beautiful, black stallions appeared.

"Wow! As simple as that!" Matt said with surprise and pleasure.

Chapter 4: Who Goes There?

They travelled the first ten miles in total silence much to the frustration of the boys; both felt the need to discuss everything that had happened to them so far. The realisation that Merlin could now be considered as a real person was one revelation but to find and see a real and living dragon was another.

Merlin's use of magic was another area that fascinated both of them and despite the fact that the travel was easy on horseback they couldn't wait for the moment they would stop, dismount and share their thoughts.

Merlin, however, had no inclination of the boys needs and didn't exactly enjoy being forced to accompany them. He had been a loner all his life, from choice as well as from the necessity to practice his magic.

During his time at Camelot he had become reclusive to his chambers and came out only when the King sought his wisdom or advice.

He missed Arthur the man more than Arthur the King; he had known him since birth and had protected him throughout his illustrious life. But the man the King had become, because of his grief, bore no resemblance to his friend and he had been reminded of the mortality and weaknesses of mankind.

The boys stopped their forward travel when they heard a thud followed by a grunt. They turned to see where the sound had come from and saw Merlin sitting on the ground and minus a horse.

"Are you all right Merlin?" James asked and dismounted to help Merlin up. "I take it we have reached the barrier you spoke of."

"You are correct and I can go no further with you at this time," he said dusting himself down. "Before I go there is something that I must give you both."

He opened a small skin pouch held shut by a drawstring.

"I have here the potion I spoke of earlier. It is tasteless but there will be some discomfort in the head whilst your mind connects with Aragon's."

He gave the pouch to James and then produced another for Matt who took it.

"Drink it now my friends for I can give you no greater friend or protector than Aragon."

The boys looked at each other for a brief moment before nodding and then downing the contents. For a few moments nothing happened and then as if in unison both clasped the sides of their heads as the first stroke of pain hit with a hammer like blow.

Their vision disappeared in an explosion of vivid colours which faded until all they saw was unbroken darkness, like that of a soot covered chimney. Then slowly a vision appeared and they saw the world from an elevated position, high, high in the sky they watched the earth move below them and they realised that they were witnessing the scene from flight. The flight of Aragon!

Again the pain shot through them and then for the first time they heard Aragon's thoughts.

You have reached the invisible barrier and Merlin must return. As nightfall arrives I will keep a vigil over you both and you may sleep knowing that you are safe for there is nothing that I cannot see in the darkness of the night.

The boys projected their thanks and were told they were welcome.

"From this moment forwards your thoughts can be passed between you and Aragon as required. He has no access to your past thoughts or memories and you have no access to his but from this moment forwards the memories and thoughts you all experience will be shared when called upon."

With the pain gone, the two of them focussed on their own surroundings and realised with surprise that Merlin had gone and they were alone. They were not without their mode of transport though and their stallions waited patiently by for them to mount.

"Just like that?" Matt asked.

"Apparently so," James responded.

Now that they were alone they could converse in the normal unrestricted fashion.

"I have to say I wasn't expecting all of this. This goes beyond my wildest dreams. Merlin, dragons; I never believed for one moment that their legends could be true and yet here we are in the thick of it again."

"Yeah, and unusually we know of our task straight away. That's a first!"

"So is having our minds linked with a dragon."

"If this was the first time that we passed through the time portal then I would be worried stiff about the goings on here. Actually, change that, I would probably be panicking. I don't feel like that at all though."

"I know what you mean and me too. This might sound strange and a bit vain but I want to see what I look like and see what ordinary men dress like around here. I have never travelled so far without seeing another human."

"Me too! There's a river up ahead if we follow it a way we might find a back pool, still enough to get a good look at our reflections."

It wasn't long before they found what they were looking for and gazed down into the depths of the pool. What they saw didn't seem to disappoint either of them.

"Pretty ordinary looking if you ask me," Matt commented.

"Nothing to write home about that's for sure, age is a little difficult to make out due to the beards but I'm betting on about thirtyish."

"I'll second that. The fact that we are average Joes in the looks department means that we are going to blend in easy enough and be able to travel without raising too many eyebrows."

"It doesn't take a genius to work out that we come from the poorer side of town judging by the clothes we are wearing."

"Perhaps, but they are clean and not in a state of complete disrepair. It could be that we are not exactly the poorest amongst the poor. I wonder what our skills are."

"We could use what we had in Sherwood if we need to, a thatcher and a smithy, which would give us an identity if we needed it."

"I meant to ask you James what period of history are we in exactly. I don't remember studying anything about King Arthur."

"Me too, but I think that's because there is little proof of Arthur being real and not just a legend, but I might be wrong about that. Something in my memory, probably internet based, is telling me about his existence was about 500BC but I could be decades off on this, maybe even centuries."

"Well it's something to go on and more than I had. What say you we keep travelling until sunset and make camp near woods that might offer a little shelter from the cool of the night?"

"Sounds like we have a plan." James replied and mounted his horse.

They travelled for another two hours and even managed to enjoy the peace and quiet of their surroundings. As the sun set so the light faded quickly and the two made their way to the edge of a small copse.

Dismounting they led the horses through slowly, as the maze of small and new saplings seemed to swallow any available space between the more mature trees. Eventually, towards the middle, they found a clearing big enough to spread their blankets down. Matt dug out a fire pit with a stout branch, while James tied their horses loosely allowing them enough freedom to move around a little.

James found some lichen and Matt took out a piece of flint and iron pyrite, he had discovered in his pocket earlier, and started to strike them together showering the lichen with hot orange sparks. The lichen started to smoulder and James gently blew on the area until a small flame burst into life. Carefully, he added some tiny twigs and then some thicker ones which caught easily. When the fire became more established Matt added some solid branches and the warmth from the burning spread while the flames lit the area sufficiently to give them good visibility in their clearing.

"We should have asked Merlin for some provisions before he left; as far as we know we have no food." James muttered feeling the first pangs of hunger since the meal with Merlin earlier that day.

"Well there are water carriers on the horses so who knows there might be something in one of those bags attached to the saddle, we never did check through them."

"Well we need to unburden the horses so let's check through the gear now."

Quickly, they unstrapped the saddles and removed them from the horse's backs. James removed the blankets and spread them out by the fire whilst Matt searched through the bags.

"There is not much here James but we have got fire starting material, spare water bladders, a couple of horn cups and yes, yes, yes, some bread and a little cheese."

"Bless you Merlin!" Matt said out loud and they both sat by the fire and shared some of the food."

"Let's keep some for tomorrow, just in case," James suggested.

"Maybe we should make a bow and a few arrows tomorrow just in case there isn't enough to keep us going. After all, we don't exactly know how far it is to the cliff castle and you are very good with the bow James."

"That is a good idea and this copse should provide us with everything we need apart from string."

"There is some sort of twine in one of the other bags; I didn't mention it because it didn't seem that important at the time, but I am sure it would do."

The darkness was complete by the time they had finished their food and the two of them lay back to rest for the night, planning to get up at first light. James fell asleep immediately as he had always been able to do but Matt watched the flames of the fire dance for a while, thinking back to the time he had experienced in Sherwood Forrest and where he had gone to sleep each night watching the camp fires.

When he finally closed his eyes a crack of snapping wood made him open them and sit up suddenly. He listened carefully trying to attune his hearing beyond the crackling of the fire in front of him. Sure enough another snapping branch broke under pressure and Matt knew that they were not alone. Gently, he shook James and when he stirred and opened his eyes Matt held his hand over James' mouth.

"What is it Matt?" James asked a little annoyed at being woken up in the manner he had just experienced.

"We are not alone; there is somebody else in the copse. I can hear moving about and the occasional branch snapping. Listen for yourself."

They listened carefully and for the third time the sound came again.

"It has to be a creature or something the horses don't appear spooked and I mean, what are the chances of somebody else being in the middle of nowhere and in the very same copse as us?"

"I am not so sure James and I know just what to do!"

With that statement Matt focussed his mind on Aragon and tried to communicate with the dragon. The answer appeared in his head immediately after his thoughts left.

"Aragon says there are two others in the copse moving stealthily toward our position. He cannot make out who they are but he cannot see any weapons accompanying them."

"You spoke to Aragon?"

"Yes, and I got his answer straight away."

Matt stood up and called out. "Who goes there?"

"What sort of question is that, you heard that from an old army film or something didn't you?" James scoffed.

"What if I did, the question seemed right for the moment."

"It didn't get an answer though did it? If our position wasn't known, it is now."

"I would imagine that with a fire like this the glow would be visible from some distance away." Matt said sharply.

Before the two could converse any further, a call come from not too far away.

"I take it back Matt, it get a response after all."

"Was that a male or a female voice, I couldn't be sure?"

"I couldn't make it out either."

Chapter 5:
Friend or Foe?

“Hello in the camp, have no fear for we are not armed and have no desire to harm you,” The voice came.

“Identify yourselves,” Matt demanded in a voice that sounded like it too came from a film.

James raised his eyes to heaven before taking over the situation.

“Come towards the fire and share it’s warmth with us,” he called in a voice more befitting of the time period.

Two characters emerged into the light cast by the fire, swathed in old and tatty blankets that were worn too thin to offer much protection from the nights chill.

"Greetings friends, I am William Farmer and this is my daughter Mary, thank you for your kindness sir."

"You are welcome friends." James replied gesturing with his hand and indicating for them to sit.

"What brings you out into the middle of nowhere so late into the evening?"

"We had no choice but to leave our land, a punishment by Sir Thomayne for having a poor harvest. In truth it was not our fault, for the crops grew with a disease that stunted the growth of them; we have no idea what caused it. Sir Thomayne's men burned down our home and forced us to go and never come back. I could not fight back for I am but a common man and have a daughter to care for which has not been easy since her mother died less than a year past."

"It sounds to me that luck hasn't smiled upon you lately," James offered.

"I haven't seen luck for her to smile," William responded.

Matt looked the pair over, they appeared to be who they said they were but he had learned from past adventures that things might not be as they seem. But they were dishevelled, looked cold, had no belongings with them and looked down on their luck.

"When was the last time you ate?" He asked gently.

"Day before yesterday."

"We have some bread and cheese if you would care for some."

"That is kind of you sir and maybe we can do something for you in return."

"There is no need for that."

The girl pulled her blanket off from her head and Matt judged her age to be about twelve. Her hair was the colour of straw, matted and unkempt but he was captivated by the colour of her eyes, a deep sapphire blue that suggested intelligence and a forthright nature. Why they suggested that he didn't really know but it was the impression he got.

She took the hunk of bread gently before stuffing a huge piece into her mouth and chewing with relish. In truth it was probably a little stale now but she didn't seem to mind.

Matt noticed that William had the same coloured eyes as his daughter; there was no doubt in his mind that the two were related. He couldn't judge the age though; the dirt on his face, the long and bushy beard did everything to hide it. That didn't worry Matt unduly, it was typical of the people of Sherwood Forest, when he had been there, so it made sense that it was like that during times further back in history. *Hygiene hasn't really been invented yet* he thought to himself grimly.

After the two guests had eaten James invited them to share their fire for the rest of the night, making up his mind to question them some more in the morning.

The last embers of the fire were still smouldering gently when he woke just after the dawn had cast the first glimpse of light on the distant horizon.

The air was damp and chilly and heavy dew clung to grassy clumps scattered intermittently around the clearing.

He stood and stretched then gently shook his friend's shoulders. Matt raised himself and stretched out his hands towards the fire remnants.

"Shall I put some more wood on?" He asked.

"Not much point, we will leave soon."

"What about these two?"

"I don't know, did you believe their story?"

"Sounds typical of the times and they certainly look the part. What about you?"

"Just had a feeling there was more that they haven't told us."

"We'll ask them when they wake."

"You can ask me now Matt if you wish, I am already awake," William interrupted before he opened his eyes. "I can't blame you for thinking like that especially as you have already been more than generous towards us. But it was late when we came across you and we, like you, had been travelling all day."

"How do you know we had been travelling all day?"

"There was still a sweat line on the horses around the saddle it was clear that you had travelled far."

"You know about horses?"

"I had two before they were seized along with my land. We used them for a lot of tasks on the land, as well for transportation of our goods. Our story is not going to change, we told you the truth, perhaps we could have given more details like the fact that we were made examples of to the other farmers because we had the most land and were the most successful amongst them. The plain truth is that all have suffered from the disease that blighted our crops but we were the only ones sanctioned for it."

James had listened carefully and watched William's face as he spoke. The man maintained eye-contact and James believed him.

"What about you two, are you knights? The horses suggest that you are wealthy men."

"No we are not knights but we are on a quest on behalf of another and we are travelling to the castle on the cliffs at the Northern Sea shore line. Do you know it?"

"Could see it from our land! It is supposed to be deserted but there are a lot of comings and goings and I know that Sir Thomayne uses it as a base from time to time. Castle Witch it is known by because it is said to be possessed by the power of one of the most evil of Witches in the region, Sargo."

"Where will you go now that you have no home?"

"Actually we have travelled too far. We were heading for the village of Two Oaks where my cousin is a blacksmith. It is just outside the lands owned by Sir Thomayne. Unfortunately, we took a wrong turn in the dark last night and have bypassed the place by a good few miles."

"Well, since we have to head in that direction, why don't you accompany us until we reach your cousins village?"

"We will be pleased to accept your offer Sir, I will wake Mary straight away."

Whilst he attended her Matt and James saddled and loaded the horses with what little they had and then kicked some soil over the last of the fire. Then the group head out of the copse and turned west.

It was four hours before the village of Two Oaks appeared in the distance and a smile formed on Williams face as he explained the layout of it and named a few of those who dwelled there.

Their arrival, and in particular the quality of the horses they arrived with, drew the entire villages attention and everybody seemed to line the main track through the village to look at them. One or two recognised William and Mary and called out greetings.

They kept going until they reached the last building on their side of the track, it was obviously the smithy. They could smell the heated metal and hear the clanging of the hammer as it shaped it. William called out his cousin's name and a huge man appeared from under the thatched but open building that lay in front of the more traditional dwelling.

William, Mary! How lovely to see you," he said hugging the girl and clasping his cousins forearm.

"Who are these fine men you travel with and what beautiful beasts, it is rare to see such quality in horses."

William introduced Matt and James and made a big deal out of the hospitality that he and Mary had been shown. Richard told them that they were not allowed to leave without having the benefit of a hot meal inside them. Matt and James accepted and were escorted into the house where a horn of some kind of ale, that offended both boy's taste buds, was given to them.

William shared the story of how he lost his land and Richard told him that the village needed more farmers and that there was plenty of land for him to rent. His relief was apparent.

Matt and James told Richard about their quest to visit Castle Witch. They told him that they journeyed to find the very man that had taken William's land because he had something that belonged to a friend of theirs but the rest of the details they left out.

"Nobody gets to go into Castle Witch not unless invited by Sir Thomayne and even then he only sees knights, not common folk," William told them.

"Maybe they need to go disguised as knights," Richard suggested.

"We can't go around and pretend we are knights, we have no armour, no squires no weapons, how could we possibly pose as knights?"

"My uncle is a blacksmith! He could make the things you need," Mary suggested shyly.

"There is more to it than just that; they would need papers, a coat of arms," William told her.

"The thought is good but it seems an awful lot of trouble to go to just to get into a castle," Matt said.

"It's the only way you are going to get in," Richard told them.

"Actually I have something else, there is a jousting tournament in the castle grounds in two weeks' time. All the main knights will be invited to stay within the castle; the perfect cover," William said eagerly.

"We can't joust, James is very good with a bow and arrow and I am not too bad with the sword."

"I can teach you how to joust, there isn't that much to it. Poise, balance, thrust and thus like. I used to squire for a knight in my younger days," Richard said excitedly. Nothing very exciting ever happens around here, this would be great."

"You said we only have two weeks, can you seriously teach us that in that time frame?"

"If you are willing, I can teach you."

"Let us think on it for a while for it's us who risk injury to limbs," Matt said.

In principal both Matt and James liked the sound of the challenge but injury was a serious concern, it could prevent them from achieving their ultimate objective. James felt that they should have a reserve plan just in case they couldn't master it but without seeing the castle even that was difficult to achieve. They discussed the issue before agreeing to try it.

Richard told them that he had a selection of armour in storage; he would need to make adjustments but they would do the job. A coat of arms was left to Mary who apparently had some skills in the art department, and as for the papers, well William knew exactly what they should look like and include and Matt and James would do the penmanship themselves. Within three days their equipment was ready and they were ready for their first jousting lesson.

Chapter 6: Preparations

At sunrise the next day a happy and excited group of travellers made their way quietly from the village keen to keep the reasons for their departure unknown.

The armour was wrapped and hidden in some sacks but there was no disguising the jousting poles until James had the idea of tying one each side of the horse and connecting them with blankets to make a type of litter.

They made their exit from the village completely unseen and James in particular was pleased that he didn't need to find explanations for their departure.

Richard kept them going for an hour until they came to a small meadow, long enough to match the length of a tournament jousting arena and far enough away from the village to avoid being seen.

William and Richard helped Matt and James with their armour, each piece being strapped onto their bodies carefully. Both the boys were shocked at the weight of it and the severe restrictions it placed on their movement but they were both physically strong and compensated for the movements by reducing the size of them. The weight was just something they were going to have to get used to.

Getting onto the horses in all of this was also difficult as the armour covering their joints was not as flexible as the joints themselves. Like everything else it was going to take a little time and practice, but time wasn't really on their side.

William led Matt to one end of the meadow whilst Richard led James to the other end. Both gave instructions to the riders and told them where on the body to aim for, before giving them the jousting lances.

Matt gripped his and held it in the vertical position before lowering it to test the weight when it was horizontal. He was glad of his rugby training for he already had developed strong wrists from all the scrum downs. The weight was fine but as he tried to move the lance left or right the length of it exaggerated the movement at the tip and he made a mental note to keep such movements subtle.

At the other end of the field James was running similar tests of his own. He had already mastered the skill of keeping his directional movements small, his skills with the bow had already taught him that a tiny movement could have a significant effect on his aim and he recognised the similarity with the jousting lance.

Finally, Richard and William left their knights and walked to a more central position in the meadow.

Mary joined them, excited and smiling broadly.

"When I drop this piece of cloth it is the signal to prepare yourselves, when the cloth hits the ground you may start your charge," Richard shouted at them and raised his arm with the cloth poised and fluttering in the gentle breeze.

Both riders lowered their visors.

He let the cloth go and it swayed to and fro as it completed its journey to the ground.

From both ends of the meadow came the shout of "Yah!" and the horses leapt into action and started to race towards one another.

Halfway across and Matt and James lowered their lances and positioned them for the attack. Within their armour the competitive spirit of the two boys threatened to explode as they prepared to meet, both were grinning delightedly and yet both would act as if their life depended upon it. All thoughts of this being training left them as they bore down on each other.

Neither flinched nor cowered, both kept their aim true and both hit each other in the centre of their torso with a calamitous scraping of wood on metal.

The two riders were flung back by the force of the impact so it looked like they were lying on their backs on the horse until they forced themselves back upright and slowed down their horses.

"Man that was a hell of a collision, amazing, I never thought that this would be so much fun," Matt shouted at James who returned the same grin.

"That was absolutely brilliant and it is going to get even better next time when I remove you from your horse Matt," James returned.

"We'll see about that, let's go for round two."

The two of them continued practicing all morning before Richard suggested that it was time to rest the horses and have something to eat. Neither Matt nor James had yet been unseated and both were justifiably proud of that. They were helped out of their armour and they flexed their limbs with pleasure at the release of the restrictions.

"I have to say that considering you two have never jousted before you seem to have a natural ability for it and I think that after a week's training you will be able to hold your own against most of your opponents but be warned you are going to come up against knights that have been doing this for years and can change the direction of their aim at the very last second. You won't see it until it hits you in a place that you might not have expected," Richard told them.

"We don't have to win the competition we just need a way into the castle," James told him.

"What exactly is it that you are trying to retrieve?" William asked.

"I am afraid that we have been sworn to secrecy and are not at liberty to discuss that with anybody. What I can tell you is that it is important and it might prevent a possible war," Matt told him.

"We haven't had a war in many years and I for one would like to keep it so, if there is anything that we can do to help you further then just ask."

"Thank you William and to be honest there is no telling at this stage exactly what we do need so we may well come asking for your assistance."

The afternoon carried on as the morning had with both boys desperately trying to unseat each other but it wasn't to be and at the close of the afternoon both had to concede a draw.

William and Richard were delighted with the way in which the two had performed and were already thinking ahead to their coat of arms.

To make things simpler it had been decided that the two should become brothers and therefore needing only one coat of arms between them. William suggested that their lions should face in the opposite direction thus giving them individuality. They liked this idea and Mary went to work on their shields painting the coats of arms for all to see.

She really was talented and James would have bet money on the work being completed by a professional artist if he hadn't of known otherwise. Then she did their banners and stitched them tightly onto the poles William had cut and shaped for her.

By the end of the second week the boys were as prepared as they could ever have been in the short time that they had to practise.

The training was complete and still, there had been an impasse between the boy's abilities and neither had been unseated.

William and Richard agreed to act as their squires and to make sure that they were not recognised both shaved their beards off. Even Mary wouldn't have recognised them if she hadn't watched them shave.

A day and a half traveling was all that remained for them to negotiate and get to their destination but, as Richard had warned them, if they were discovered impersonating knights the penalty would be certain death. They made up their mind to change the direction of their course and approach the castle from the south where there were very few people living. This meant that they would reach the castle virtually unseen.

On route, during periods of rest, Richard gave Matt and James some help to improve their swordsmanship. Matt already had some experience with the sword, but with a lighter version that the one they carried now.

In their armour, and with the heavyweight swords, the fighting was remarkably slow. If you put your effort into a full-blooded swing then it took a few seconds to re-position it for the next attack. Similarly, if you parried a blow, the force of the momentum had the same effect. It was like fighting in slow motion and Matt enjoyed it more than James, but to be fair, his physique was more suited to it. The training was useful though and both boys benefitted from Richard's knowledge and skills.

On the morning of the second day of travel the Northern sea came into their view from the top of a gentle incline and with it came the first glimpse of Castle Witch.

"That is your destination you two, not exactly the most hospitable looking of places is it?" Richard said pointing at it.

"From here it doesn't look as if it is still habitable," Matt said ruefully.

"There is about a quarter of it, the furthest quarter away from the sea that is still usable. I have been in their a few times in the past when the harvest has been completed and the stores are being replenished. It is as miserable a castle on the inside as it looks on the outside. I have never liked it," William told them.

"What about all this witchcraft stuff and the wicked Witch herself, Sargo?" James asked.

"There is definitely something to the stories. Sargo has been seen in the castle on several occasions and it is rumoured that she reads the future for Sir Thomayne. I think that this is why he is always successful in the things he chooses to do.

"I have no doubt in my mind that it was she who brought disease to our crops this year but I know of nothing that she could possibly gain from ridding the land of me and Mary.

"There have been cases of strange celebrations at the castle which have put fear into some of the servants there. If that is not enough to be aware of, then there have been several cases of people that have disappeared; never to be seen again. I am not sure if that could be attributed to magic or perhaps punishment from Sir Thomayne. He has been known to throw some people, who have displeased him, off the cliff tops and onto the rocks below."

"He sounds like such a nasty character," James said ruefully.

"It's more than that, the man is evil, possible as evil as the Witch that serves him."

"Well if all goes well we can get what we have come for and then report his involvement to the King and he can take care of him. I think the less direct involvement we have with him the better," James said with a frown of concern."

"Even if we do have a few problems with him we have tricks and surprises up our own sleeves that we can use if necessary," Matt added.

"What might those be?" William enquired.

"Now if I told you that they wouldn't be surprises now would they?" Matt grinned.

They moved off the incline and started travelling once more and as they descended towards the coastline the castle disappeared temporarily from view and James felt a sense of relief. He wasn't one to unduly worry or even fear anything but this place had something about it, a hidden quality, an unpleasantness, something evil and he couldn't prevent the feeling of dread that crept through him. Somehow he knew right then that this quest was not going to run smoothly and that they would face some real tests before they succeeded. He wished Merlin had been able to come but knew that the wish was pointless. Anyway, they still had Aragon and nobody knew about him.

Chapter 7:
Castle Witch

Late that afternoon, they finally reached the castle and the two acting squires led James and Matt through the portcullis and they entered the lair of Sir Thomayne.

There was little to see as the place seemed mostly deserted. Buildings built around the castle walls held horses and there was the occasional stable hand on duty to be seen but the buildings skirting the castle ruins were abandoned and in truth, judging by their state of disrepair, were empty for good reason.

A second portcullis loomed and four soldiers guarded it. One raised his hand to halt the band. Richard took the lead.

"I present Sir Matthew and Sir James of the House of Morbridge from the county of Northumbria."

"Welcome Sir Matthew and Sir James. This is as far as you can travel with the horses and squires. If you would do me the courtesy of dismounting they will be given a space on the outer wall where the horses can be tended."

Matt and James did as requested and dismounted, nodding at the others to go with the soldier.

The one who had spoken before spoke again.

"You are here for the tournament I assume and if you are, then there are entry papers to sign before you will be given accommodation for the duration of it."

"Lead us forward so that we might attend these tiresome trivialities," James said opting for a sense of bored aloofness.

"Follow me my Lords."

Each signed the necessary entry form and the guard looked at them in surprise.

"Only the jousting My Lords. Do you not wish to test your skills with the archery and sword?"

"Oh very well, Sir Matthew will take the sword challenge and I the archery," James said in the same bored manner.

After submitting the extra paperwork, they were led deeper into the castle through partially destroyed corridors, open to the outside elements, until they came to an area of the castle apparently untouched by the ruin. Still they kept moving forward until a succession of doors lay open along a lengthy and unusually wide corridor.

"Do you wish separate accommodation my Lords or do you wish to share, we don't get to many brothers entering the competitions?"

"We will share thank you." Matt said and entered through the door that the soldier indicated.

"I will have my men bring in a second bed in just a few moments my Lords," The soldier said and barked out a quick order.

Two men disappeared into the next room and came back carrying a fully prepared bed. Matt and James moved aside to allow them to bring it in. After they had set it in its new position one of the men went to the great hearth and lit the fire from one of the torches. The wood there had already been coated with something and fire spread across the hearth instantly. The two men disappeared.

The remaining soldier informed them that dinner would be announced by the blast of a horn and a man would be sent to guide them and introduce them to Sir Thomayne. James thanked the man and he left shutting the door behind him. They were alone at last.

"What did you make of all that?" Matt asked his friend.

"I don't believe that this is anything out of the ordinary but this castle is. I have never seen such an inhospitable place. There is more going on here than meets the eye for sure. "

"Did you notice that there wasn't any sign of an arena for this tournament outside the castle grounds?"

"I did and that leads me to believe that the tournament is either being held elsewhere or here within the grounds. From outside, the castle looks massive, easy large enough to hold an arena somewhere."

"I suspect you are right. I am looking forward to seeing and meeting our host later and getting an idea of just what we are up against here."

"What worries me is that we don't have a clue as to who his allies are. There might be many knights present here but which are independent, just here for the tournament, and which are tied to him with some twisted sense of loyalty or fear."

"We have a couple of days to work that out before the tournament starts and I for one will be watching very carefully," Matt answered ruefully.

"We need to get Richard and William on the same task, they might be able to find out more from the other squires than we can from the knights."

"That's a good point and Mary would probably have quite a free reign over the place, not having too many duties, I wonder just what she might find out."

"We can see to these matters in the morning for I don't think we shall see them before."

"You've already started to talk like one of them, you seem to adapt very easily to the roles you have to play," Matt grinned.

"I've noticed the same with you. We're getting good at improvising, maybe we should join the drama club at school when the term starts."

"What and be the laughing stock of our team mates? No chance!" They both laughed.

The blast of a horn sounded easily through the thick oak door announcing that dinner was ready and they waited for the knock that they had been told to expect. It came and Matt opened the door. A middle aged man in old, simple, cloth clothing, that clearly needed to be replaced, stood at the other side. The servant did not appear to be well looked after.

"I am your guide to the banqueting hall my Lords if you would care to follow me," He said in a croaky voice.

Matt nodded and told him to lead on and they followed him down a succession of corridors until the space opened up into a great hall that was filled with tables, men and a variety of entertainers, including dancers, acrobats and jesters.

The servant stopped at the entrance and bellowed the arrival of Sir Matthew and Sir James before leading them in to a table to the right of where Sir Thomayne sat, his presence made obvious by the quality of the clothes he wore and the displayed banner showing his coat of arms behind him. Their host stood and raised his vessel toward them.

"We have not had the pleasure of meeting before and indeed I have never heard of the house that you represent, but eat your fill and consider yourselves welcome at Castle Witch. I look forward to assessing your skills at the tournament arena."

Both Matt and James raised their drinking vessels and thanked their host for the generosity they had received and then sat down.

Two more knights already sat at their table and Matt introduced himself and then his brother. The two men were from the south and were also related, only a little more distantly that Matt and James.

One of the two introduced himself as Sir Henry and his cousin as Sir Harold and a casual, but no less friendly, conversation broke out between the small group.

Every now and again proceedings were halted by the arrival of another knight who was shown the same courtesy and respect as they had been and James in particular made mental notes to remember as much of the detail that was given. Additionally, he kept a close eye on Sir Thomayne and the three other knights seated alongside him. These were surely his most trusted comrades.

Both he and Matt pretended to drink as much of the wine and ale that their table companions downed but in reality they had scarcely touched a drop by the time the other two were becoming loud and boisterous from the effects of it.

James had waited for that to happen before he started to question the two about the men at Sir Thomayne's table. He was not surprised when he learned that one of them was Sir Humphrey, another knight of the round table. There had to be somebody else from Camelot here, it just made sense that Thomayne had an associate from there.

The other two were fairly local to Castle Witch territory and Sir Guy and Sir Terrence were Thomayne's nearest neighbours.

Both men were described as mercenaries without a degree of loyalty or compassion for anyone or anything and were to be avoided in the tournament if possible. They had reputations to deliberately hurt and maim other knights for the pleasure of it.

Matt and James were glad when the knights started to return to their rooms and as they rose the servant who had brought them there appeared to take them back.

Matt picked up a huge piece of chicken breast to take with him and promptly gave it to the servant when he left. The grateful man placed it in a grubby pocket and murmured his appreciation. He told them that he would call them after dawn so that they might prepare for the day's practice and then he left leaving the boys alone.

"Well that was interesting; we have been introduced to our enemy and know of at least three accomplices that are probably involved with him," Matt said pleased with what they had found out already.

"We don't know if Sir Guy and Sir Terrance had anything to do with the taking of Excalibur but I would bet money that they would be the first to support Thomayne if the need arrived.

"Sir Humphrey, on the other hand, I am sure played a part in the robbery. The four of them would make a very formidable enemy if we had to face them all at one time and I would hazard a guess that there were other knights in that hall that would rally to his side."

"I agree and we are going to have to be very careful that we never get into such a position, better to face them one on one."

"Well, we have a couple of days of practise before the tournament starts and I vote that, apart from that, we find out as much about this place as we can and the people that inhabit it. Against such numbers the only ally we have is the knowledge we gain."

The two of them settled down for a night's sleep but neither slept that well, each caught up in the worry and difficulty of the task they had come here for. In the morning they rose and when the servant appeared.

They were led out to where their horses had been quartered for the foreseeable future and grinned widely at the two men who already were hard at work brushing the beautiful creatures down. They exchanged pleasantries before William suggested that they leave the castle to practise.

"It makes sense not to show your opponents too much of your skills and beside we need to find some privacy to tell you what we found out last night."

"That sounds very interesting William, it sounds like you had a good evening."

"For finding out information yes, but in terms of realising what we are up against, whatever it is that you want will not be easy and the strength of the opposition is considerable. The presence of another that strikes the fear of death, complicates matters further."

"Sargo is here isn't she?" James asked.

"How did you know?"

"Why face some of the enemy when you can face them all," James said sarcastically.

William was uncertain as to what James meant by that so he deigned to contribute further to the discussion. He started to saddle up the horses and Richard came to help.

The lances were collected and the armour and the small group left the castle grounds at a slow and leisurely pace. Mary skipped alongside Matt's horse humming in a carefree manner which brought an ironic smile to his face. *She wouldn't be singing if she knew of the difficulty of what they had to do,* he thought but was glad that her ignorance of the situation brought at least her some peace.

Chapter 8:
Sargo

They were a mile away from the castle before James broke the silence and asked what they knew about Sargo.

"Most of what I know is hearsay, bits and pieces collected over the years, told by many different people over too much ale. Here's what I have. It's said that Sargo wasn't always evil; in fact she is supposed to have started out as a good Witch, if you can believe that. As far as I am concerned a Witch is a Witch and good riddance to all of them.

"Something happened to her in her infancy as a Witch. Apparently, she tried to defend a knight and rid him of a spell cast by another. Unfortunately the other Witch was stronger, more powerful and cast a spell on Sargo in retribution for her interference. The spell has remained and Sargo remains as the type of Witch whose mission in life is to cause chaos and misery.

"She has lived for centuries and joins forces, from time to time, with other unsavoury characters who have evil intentions but do not have the power of magic. She trades her service for their souls in a deal that cements their fate after death. Her victims are unable to find their way to the afterlife and as such, are forced to remain in limbo between the living world and the spiritual one.

"Whilst she is in partnership with a member of the living, the more evil she commits the more her strength and power gains. She is thought to be one of the most powerful Witches in the land and her power is said to rival that of Merlin's. She can read the future and can see all around her even if she does not appear to be present." William told them ruefully.

"Is there anything anybody can do to rid her of the spell she suffers from or alternatively anything that could dispossess her of her powers?" James asked.

"It is said that only the fire breath of a dragon can release her from the confines of the spell and alas the dragons are all extinct now, killed by the glory seekers who had little else to do but hunt and destroy."

James' spirits lifted a little when he heard the last statement. There was hope after all and she wasn't infallible, at least not any more. But Aragon was still young, not yet fully grown, did he really have the ability to relieve her of the spell. James couldn't answer that but his natural optimism carried the glimmer of hope.

"So what of her at Castle Witch William?"

"Richard and I saw her last night in the small hours before dawn, the air was thunderous, I couldn't sleep and my head was pounding. I thought we were in for a huge storm. But alas it didn't come. At the peak, when my head was aching the worst, I ventured from my quarters deciding to fetch some cool water from the well. Richard joined me suffering from the same problems. When we reached the well we heard the sound of approaching footsteps and both of us hid behind the stonework of the well.

"Sargo passed right by us, along with Sir Thomayne, they were deep in conversation but I couldn't hear what it was all about. There was just enough light for me to see her face. She does not look as you would expect a Witch to look. She is young, with straw coloured hair as fine as silk and her beauty is beyond compare."

"How could you be sure that it was her?"

"As she passed us by the ache in my head subsided and completely disappeared when she left my line of sight. I examined the sky and it was clear, there was no moon but there were no clouds. The ache in my head was caused by her presence not the arrival of storm clouds. Richard experienced the same."

"It would appear that something else must be going on and I would wager a bet that it has something to do with King Arthur and Camelot," Matt interjected.

"It could be a plot to assassinate King Arthur and take over Camelot;

"If Thomayne has the power of the Witch on his side then there is no telling what he might accomplish," William said softly.

"There is a good spot ahead for us to commence our training," Richard said changing the subject.

As they reached it Matt and James started to practice sparing with the heavy swords. Matt was clearly the stronger and defeated James in the spar by knocking his sword from his hand. James practiced with the bow for a while before the horses were readied for the jousting.

Richard and William helped the boys into the rest of their armour so that they were fully protected from potential injury and then led their respected knights to the ends of the practice area.

Satisfied that they were totally prepared the two squires left them for the centre of the run and then moved back from the collision site.

Richard took out a piece of cloth and told the boys to be ready. At the drop of the cloth they charged. The thud of the horses hooves in the soft ground intensified as the two closed in on each other. At twenty metres apart they raised their lances and held them steady just in time to connect them with each other's armour. The sound of the collision echoed around the rolling hills as they slowed near the end of their run and turned. Neither Matt nor James had been sent into the horizontal position after the impact. Both had taken it full on but twisted at the vital moment, allowing the lances to skid off their armour.

Two more runs occurred before, at the end of the third, James felt a dull ache in his head. He immediately attributed it to the blows that had been imposed upon him by Matt, but the pain started to get worse and forced him to raise the visor on his helmet.

On the other side of the run Matt was experiencing the same pain and had lifted his visor too. James urged his horse to the centre of their makeshift arena and dismounted. William took the reins.

"Can you feel that?" William asked grimacing.

James nodded his response as Matt rode in and dismounted.

"This is what we felt last night. If I am not mistaken Sargo is close by."

They turned to look in the opposite direction from where they were facing and sure enough two horses, with riders approached. Since they approached from in front of the sun it was difficult to make out who the riders were. The glare of the sun turned the form of the two incoming riders into silhouettes, but also added to the throbbing in their heads.

The travellers were on top of them before they could clearly make out their features; Sir Thomayne and the most beautiful woman that Matt and James had ever seen; Sargo.

"Good afternoon Sir Matthew, Sir James, I trust the new day finds you well.

"Good afternoon Sir Thomayne, My Lady. The day does find us well as I hope it does you?

"Allow me to present the Lady Sargo my special guest and prize giver at the forthcoming tournament.

"Your beauty would grace the finest summer day my lady and I hope I am lucky enough to be on the receiving end of one of the prizes," Matt said warmly.

"You are too kind sir." She responded smiling.

"How is it that you prefer to practise out here rather than in the arena at the castle?" Thomayne asked curious as to their motives.

"The reason is simple my Lord, we just do not wish our competitors to learn about our strengths and weaknesses," James replied.

"But surely you deprive yourself an opportunity to witness your opponent's strengths and weaknesses."

"That may be the case sir but we have no such need and they will fall from the aim of our lances."

"I am not sure, Sir James if those words are spoken by a very arrogant or very confident man."

"It is confidence I promise Sir Thomayne."

Sir Thomayne grinned. "I like that in a man and I hope your confidence is well placed and that you live up to your promise. I shall look forward to watching you compete in the first round and will observe with interest. Now, unfortunately my guest and I have to leave, we will see you at tonight's feast. Good day to you good knights."

"Good day to you both," James and Matt echoed.

They watched them ride slowly away noticing how the thudding in their heads reduced as the distance between them increased.

After practice Matt asked William and Richard to take their equipment back to the castle and apologise for their forthcoming absence at tonight's feast. When William questioned as to the reasons why Matt just said that they had business to attend to. Richard didn't look too pleased at being dismissed without a proper reason being given but William collected the amour and lances up and called Richard to help before he could question further.

Matt and James mounted up and moved away from the area heading towards a small wood a mile or so distant.

"Do you want to tell me what's going on with you Matt?"

"Of course and it's simple really. I want to make contact with Merlin, let him know what we have found out so far and see if he has any further news for us."

"How exactly do you propose to do that?"

"I am going to call in Aragon and ask him to pass the message on since Merlin cannot enter Thomayne's lands."

Reaching the wood, they entered and head for the very heart of it to ensure that they wouldn't be seen. Matt dismounted first and sat down in a small clearing. James joined him. Then Matt closed his eyes and concentrated with all his might on Aragon and called for his presence within the confines of his mind. He received his answer a moment later.

"Why do you call me when I am already here? Look above you."

Both of them heard the answer, as clearly as if it had been spoken, and immediately looked up. There on the stout branch of a young oak tree sat Aragon. He dropped down to the ground flaring his wings to slow his descent and achieve a soft landing.

"There is no need to call me like a man calls a dog. I can read your thoughts from a great distance and already know everything you have discovered thus far,"

"Sorry Aragon but we had no idea how our communication would work exactly. If you already know what we have learned, what news is there from Merlin?"

"There is little news for you except to warn you about Sargo and there is little need of that for I can sense the healthy respect you have for her. You are aware that I have the ability to end her evil powers but in order to do that the circumstances must be right. I must envelop her in fire at exactly midnight for my flames to have the desired effect. A moment sooner, or later, and although her powers will be reduced she will not lose the evil from inside her."

"In that case we need to plan that in advance so that we all can be ready," Matt said grimly.

"There are several things that will have to be timed for the right moment, the retrieving of the sword, reducing her powers, diminishing an army that Thomayne is building ready to attack Camelot amongst other things. Her powers are the most important consideration for whilst she still has them Merlin cannot help us. Now I must go."

With that the great beast ascended into the tree above and disappeared from view.

Chapter 9: Tournament

Two days later the boys sat in their room frustrated and disappointed with themselves. Since speaking with Aragon they had discovered nothing that would help them retrieve Excalibur and indeed, they hadn't even found its current location yet.

Sargo had been very elusive too, and even Richard and William, who from their position near the portcullis could see all the comings and goings to the castle, had seen nothing of her.

Sir Thomayne had been equally reclusive and hadn't even been at dinner last night; the night before the start of his tournament. Most considered his absence rude but this was his tournament and his castle so he was entitled to do as he wished.

"Tell you what Matt, I am glad that the tournament starts now, I feel the need to let off a little aggression."

"I know how you feel James and I am going in with all guns blazing, so to speak."

"Well it's time, let's go and get our horses and squires."

They no longer used the servant that had showed them around the first night and they made their own way down to the stable area where William, Richard and Mary waited for them.

The horses had been well brushed and their adornments shone after the polishing they had received. Never, had two horses looked grander. Matt commented that if a prize had been issued for the best horse then they would surely have won it.

The two squires helped them on with their armour and they were finally ready. They mounted and Richard and William led them to the area where the knights gathered. They were to march through the arena in pairs being announced to the waiting crowd who looked forward to seeing or choosing their favourite.

Thirty-two knights had entered the tournament and Matt and James lined up in eleventh and twelfth position and waited for the column to start moving. Each of the knights had their squire holding on to the horses bit trying to keep them calm amidst the noisy crowd of impatient spectators. And then it began.

Horns sounded over the noise and the first two horses and riders moved forward with an announcer shouting out their names to the cheers of the crowd. The second pairing moved forward and the whole process repeated itself. Finally, the moment they had been waiting for, James and Matt started forward. Two coloured sheets that hid the line of knights from the crowd were parted and James and Matt rode out into the arena.

"Introducing Sir Matthew and his brother Sir James of the House of Morbridge in the county of Northumbria," the announcer called out and the crowd cheered loud and enthusiastically.

"Where did all these people come from, we haven't exactly seen many villages around here?" James questioned.

"Beats me, I haven't a clue but this is a great crowd to compete in front of."

They continued forward until they reached the knights that had moved off before them and where all the jousters turned to face the crowd, and in particular, the royal box. Although there were no members of royalty present, the box had been filled with Sir Thomayne, Sargo and an entourage of unknown men and women.

When all the horses were lined up the horns blasted a monotone and the crowd fell silent. Sir Thomayne stood.

"Greetings and welcome to the fourth annual Thomayne Tournament. The knights that have been announced and paraded before you stand ready to receive the draw as picked by the lovely Lady Sargo.

Each knight is to follow the lead at the sound of his name to the preparation enclosures at either end of the arena. The draw is finite and will not be changed."

The draw began and Sargo drew a piece of parchment from a small cloth bag which held the name of all the knights. She read it out and the knight moved to the associated area. James got called early on and was matched against Sir Wilfred of Wessex whilst Matt had to wait almost to the end before being matched up against Sir Lawrence of Chester. He was led to the opposite end of the arena to James.

Many of the Knights were entered in several competitions, with swords, and bows and arrows and it was these that started the day's events off. James shot his arrows accurately against some soldiers; this was the only competition to involve anybody outside the rank of knighthood. He went through easily, outscoring his opponents with every arrow he fired.

Matt had his first fight with the sword against a formidable and larger knight. He eventually won through but it took all his strength and guile to defeat his opponent who was a strong favourite of the crowd. The crowds allegiance was fickle though and they switched their alliance to Matt when he was announced the victor of the round.

Then as the early rounds completed the knights prepared for the jousting to start. The crowd sensed the start was near and began to get even more vocal, and when the announcement for the first joust was made they cheered and the noise was deafening.

The rules were simple. A hit to the body produced a point and an unseating gave the outright win. There were three rounds.

The first few jousts were quick affairs with knights being unseated in the first run and James was only just ready in time for his bout.

"I've seen this man practicing James; he favours a target high on the torso which can easily slip to the neck. He aims to unseat every time in this manner. If you are hit in the neck there is no doubt that you will be unseated. However, he holds his lance up too high and it is easy for you to target below. If you can use your reach and connect with him a fraction before he connects with you he will not be able to resist the forward motion of his head as his lower body moves back. This will cause his lance hand to drop slightly and with the usual twist of your body you can force the lance away," William told him.

"Thank you William I will bear all that in mind."

James moved his mount into the start position and listened to the announcer call out his and his opponent's names. The starter held a coloured cloth high above his head and shouted for them to charge the second it hit the ground. As he let it go a freak gust of wind from the sea lifted it even higher and the crowd gasped as it doubled the dropping height. A silent hush came over the crowd as they waited for it to fall and kiss the ground.

James grinned with amusement at a most unusual occurrence but did not break the concentration he had on the cloth. His opponent started his run a full second before the cloth touched the ground and the crowd booed their disapproval. James still waited and started on cue.

He felt no fear as his mount charged forward and the adrenalin in his body flooded. With the intense concentration that he was used to applying in a rugby scrum, he lowered his lance at precisely the right moment and thrust his arm forward landing the tip exactly where he had aimed for and a split second before his opponent's lance now slipped harmlessly by. The force of his blow lifted the unfortunate knight clean from his seat and dumped him flat on his back on the arena floor. The crowd roared and James let out a roar of his own as he slowed his horse down and turned. He waved to the crowd as he walked casually back to the preparation area and a smiling William.

"Well done Sir Knight, exactly to plan I'd say."
James took off his helmet and grinned back at William nodding his agreement. He was a little disappointed that he would not get a second and third run but for him,

his day's work was done and he was able to watch Matt dispose of his opponent in much a similar way.

The second day of the tournament went the same way as the first but on the third day Sir Thomayne brought out a surprise guest. Excalibur. He wielded it around his head for all to see and then thrust it into the arena ground so that all the competing knights would see it at close quarters when they fought their respective competitions. It was a bold declaration of his mostly unsaid intentions and both Matt and James thought it was a show of arrogance.

All the knights recognised the sword and knew without doubt that King Arthur was no longer the only man capable of using it in battle. Some were shocked, some surprised, but a few grinned in delight for they knew exactly what was to come and the purpose of it being displayed.

James and Matt assessed the reaction of each knight as they paraded through the arena and passed the sword. They knew that they would be up against a significant number if they were to complete their mission. There was little they could do at that moment though, for they had competitions to compete in.

James, for the third day running, easily disposed of his opposition with the bow and Matt had a similar result with the sword. Now though it was time for the quarter finals of the jousting and there was a strong possibility that Matt might be drawn against James. It didn't happen but both drew very strong opponents and favourites with the crowd.

Matt was up first and the joust went the full distance. In the first two runs both Matt and his opponent had scored direct hits that scored two points each. If the third round was also drawn then Sir Thomayne would have the task of announcing a winner.

Matt already knew that his opponent had Thomayne's favour, he had seen the man take his place on Thomayne's table so he knew that the decision, if needed, would not be given to him.

He had to win outright but the task was difficult. His opponent had a longer reach than him and would get the strike in first. He didn't flinch at the last minute like some of his earlier opponents either. No, he needed something new, something a little different, something that would catch his opponent completely by surprise.

Matt lined up for the third round and waited for the signal. He knew exactly what he was going to do.

The cloth hit the ground and he charged. He judged his moment carefully then lifted his seat out of the saddle and twisted his body over so that his thigh was now seated on the saddle and his body was lined up to the far edge of the horse. His opponent missed with the lance completely whilst Matt rammed his in hard. Metal and wood sang as they met together and wooden shards flew in random directions.

Matt knew that he had done it. The relief coursed through him because the slightest hit from his opponent would have sent him flying off his horse instead.

His opponent rode back toward him.

"I have never seen anybody use that tactic Sir Matthew. Well played sir, well played indeed."

Matt nodded his thanks at the gracious nature of the Knight he had just defeated and the crowd roared at his victory.

James didn't have quite such a difficult contest and joined Matt in the semi-finals. After the Joust finished for the day. Sir Thomayne came and retrieved Excalibur from the ground and laid it on a cushion held by a servant. He whispered instructions and the servant moved away. James looked at William.

“Do you think Mary could follow to see where the sword is being taken too?”

William gave her some quick instructions of his own and she quickly disappeared.

“I wondered what your true purpose was in coming here and now I know. You came for the sword didn’t you?”

“It needs to be returned to its true owner.” James said with conviction.

“Yes it does.”

“Mention this to nobody.” James warned.

Chapter 10: Super Sleuth

Mary was an intelligent child who was used to working hard and knew her place in the world of adults. She had learned, during her short life, that children didn't get involved in the world of men and that she was better off in the background.

She had mastered the habit so well that she could be in the same room as a group of adults and yet go completely unnoticed by them.

She knew she would be able to follow the servant discretely and even as she started she remained a sensible distance behind. There was always a chance that the man she pursued could turn off and she would miss it. She had learned to use all of her senses independently as part of survival in a harsh world. Her hearing was particularly keen and she could focus on it alone and intently if required.

The servant wasn't trying to be quiet and made more than enough noise for her to follow. He made his way through a side entrance to the castle from the arena and Mary entered shortly after and followed the man though a great hall that had succumbed to ruin some time ago.

Parts of one wall and the roof had been destroyed and blackened charred sections of beam highlighted the fact that a great fire had occurred there at some time in the past.

A door at the far end, already opened, held a flight of stone steps that went in both an upward and downward direction. The servant descended the flight which in turn led to a long and winding corridor. Mary followed silently, her bare feet barely making the slightest scuffing sound as she padded along.

Another door led to another stone stairway descending even further into the bowels of the castle. It was lit dimly by the occasional torch fire.

The steps here were worn and in places almost completely eroded away. Mary took her time being careful not to disturb any of the rubble that had collected on either side of each step and betray her presence. The steps seemed to go on down forever until she finally reached the horizontal path at the bottom.

The corridor here was more like a tunnel that had been carved out of the living rock, chisel and hammer marks were clear to see by each of the torches held by brackets on the walls.

Ancient oak doors started to appear on her left and right and she knew beyond doubt that these were some sort of dungeons where prisoners could be locked up for an eternity and few would know of their existence. One such door lay open and she risked a peep inside but the space was completely dark and she couldn't make out anything.

Then the footsteps ahead of her ceased and she heard a door open. She continued cautiously forward until she could see the door the servant had entered. Draft exuded from the entrance and washed over her in a caress of silk.

She could not risk remaining her side of the doorway knowing that the servant would eventually return the way he had come. Instead she moved on beyond it grabbing a fleeting glance in as she passed.

She saw the servant lay the sword down on an embroidered cloth covered table to the side of the space. The overhanging cloth fluttered in the breeze that came from the vast opening at the rear of the space. It was completely open to the sea and whatever elements the weather threw at it.

She passed just in time as the servant straightened from his task and started to turn. Mary hid around a slight bend in the tunnel and hoped beyond all hope that the servant did not continue his original course. She heard the door shut but there was no sound of a key locking it, and then she breathed deeper as the footprints audibly started to fade and she knew for certain that the man she had followed had returned the way he'd come.

Carefully, she returned to the door and opened it. The hinges had been well oiled and despite the thickness and weight of the door it opened easily. She slipped inside and examined the surroundings. Apart from the table there was a crudely fashioned bed frame devoid of any mattress or coverings. There was nothing else.

She made her way to the edge of the opening and looked out. The daylight was already fading but she caught her breath when she looked down and realised how high up she was and how far the drop went down the face of the sheer cliffs. At the bottom, jagged rocks were being beaten by an angry sea.

Looking out, to the left and right of the room, she could make out a series of other spaces alongside. Three such spaces along, a bright light gave it a glow of warmth and Mary knew that somebody was in there and for some reason she needed to investigate further.

She left the room and shut the door quietly behind her and moved back along the tunnel toward the door that entered the illuminated space. Placing her ear to the door, she listened. A strange and eerie chanting came from inside that compelled her to enter. The lure became stronger and stronger until she found herself opening the door. She was powerless to stop herself.

A figure in a full length burgundy robe, complete with hood, stood hunched over a large stone vessel of water, or at least water is what it looked like. The vessel had been carved into the rock at one side of the room.

Mary stopped pushing at the door and watched, through the six centimetre wide gap, the figure periodically drop things into the liquid. Each time an item from the hand was released, the figure sang with an eerie and unearthly sound. She could not understand any of the words and thought a foreign language was being used. The voice was unmistakably female though, and the figure straightened after dropping an item and then stooped again to drop the next one.

Mary continued to watch and listen, unable to move from the trance like state she had fallen under. Then as the woman bent over yet again a lock of beautiful fine golden hair fell from the side of the robes hood. Mary saw it and immediately distinguished the figure it belonged too. Sargo.

The shock of her realisation snapped her senses back to reality and she retreated, carefully pulling at the door but not quite closing it. Moving quickly along the tunnel and up the ruined stairway she retraced her footsteps to the great hall.

She had the presence of mind to peer around the entrance before venturing into it and just managed to avoid being discovered by Sir Thomayne and three other knights who were talking amiably about the afternoons jousting.

Wagers were being made with explanations for their choices and there was laughter and an element of teasing between them. The noise was sufficient for Mary to skip past the entrance and follow the corridor in the opposite direction.

She felt her first pang of fear as she entered another area of the castle that she hadn't visited before and this time she had nobody to follow.

Following her instincts she ignored the few doors that she passed before the corridor came to an abrupt end and she stood in front of a larger entrance that was sealed by two huge doors.

Her spirits fell as she realised that this was as far as she could go. There had to be something huge on the other side of this doorway or there would be no need of such substantial doors. She didn't want to risk opening them and instead made her way back the way she had come.

After a few steps she heard the sound of feet on stone and voices. A group was coming her way and she recognised Thomayne's voice amongst them. She was trapped between them and the doors.

Again, Mary changed direction, the choice was simple; she couldn't get caught by Thomayne.

Approaching them, she turned the great handle and pushed. Nothing moved and her eyes widened in panic as behind her, the voices were getting closer by the second. She tried the handle on the second door and this time it turned. She pushed and the door opened a few centimetres. She pushed harder and slipped falling heavily to the ground. The fall was fortunate, as inside the huge room, several heads turned towards the door as it opened but, low to the ground, she remained unseen.

Crawling through the small gap, she entered the biggest kitchen area she had ever seen. She moved to the side just as the door swung open further and Thomayne and the same group of men that he had been wagering with entered.

The fully open door concealed her presence and she peeked around the edge of it looking for an obvious escape route but she could see none.

Thomayne moved forward and started to inspect some of the food that was being prepared for the evening feats. He clubbed a poor wretch that got in his way as he marched his way through. His sidekicks laughed and followed his path.

Mary took a chance and crawled from behind the door and went back through it holding her breath. She waited for a cry that would alert her that she had been seen but none came. Standing upright, she hurried back along the corridor to the ruined hall and this time she was in luck. It was empty and she passed quickly through and into the fresh air beyond.

Blending in with the mass of humanity that was still present from the tournament she made her way back to the stables where they all waited for her return. She ran to her father and buried her head into him. He embraced her, sympathetic to her need, and waited for her heavy breathing to subside before encouraging her to sit down and tell her story.

She told it clearly, without exaggeration and without omitting any of the details and they all commented upon how brave she had been, especially when she had nearly been caught.

Then the group discussed all that they had learned and a plan started to formulate. The night of the semi-finals was going to be a memorable night for sure but this group had no intention of celebrating the jousting.

Matt and James stayed up late discussing their options well into the night before deciding to leave the castle to meet up with Aragon once more to pass on information. Even though they could communicate by thought alone both Matt and James preferred the more normal method of face to face discussion.

They chose not to leave in secret though and took their horses out from the stables and made their way to the portcullis. The guards there challenged them and they spun them a yarn about their needing to exercise their horses who would not settle.

"They need to be in top condition for their semi-final matches," Matt explained.

"Your horses are from good breeding stock and are amongst the finest present, it is not surprising that they are a little more highly strung than most of the others. It is the price you often pay for quality," The soldier replied.

"You know your horses." Matt flattered the soldier and he and James passed through the gate.

Chapter 11: Planning

They rode in silence for some distance aiming for the same area of woodland where they had met Aragon before. Even though it was as dark a night as it could be, James didn't want to risk meeting Aragon in the open. He waited until they reached a small clearing close to the centre of the woods before he concentrated his mind on connecting with Aragon. Suddenly, moving out of the shadows, the reply came and Aragon made an appearance.

"What is on your mind?" The voice came into both Matt and James' heads simultaneously.

"We have located the whereabouts of Excalibur." James replied and proceeded to tell Aragon all that had happened.

"We thought we might try to snatch it tomorrow evening whilst the feasting and celebration is taking place for the two knights that make it into the final," James informed him.

"You have a plan?"

"Not really, not yet but we are going to work on it in the morning."

"If you succeed in getting Excalibur out of the castle you need to ensure that it is not discovered for several hours so that you might have a chance of a placing a fair distance between you and the castle.

"Bear in mind that Sargo has the power to track you in whatever direction you flee and she will not have to leave the castle to do it."

"Is there something you can do to help cover our escape?" Matt asked.

"Possibly, but you have to consider that it is not just you two that need to escape. If you leave William, Mary and Richard behind they are sure to be punished for your deceit."

"We haven't forgotten Aragon. We will return to the castle and sleep on it but can we contact you nearer to the castle, preferably somewhere where you could remain undetected."

"I have powers of my own that few are aware of but you should know that you do not need my physical presence in order to communicate with me. It can all be done in the mind."

"I'm bothered by the fact that Sargo is powerful enough to intercept any mental communication. Face to face communication like this seems more private," James expressed his concern.

"You are right to fear the extent of her powers but if she could do what you suspect then she would open her mind to me and I would know. I do not think that she can do this at the moment but perhaps you are right and we should take the precaution of discussion in this manner just in case."

"Any news from Merlin?"

"Merlin has worked continuously since your departure to try and rid the spell that prevents him from being at your side. As yet he has made no breakthrough but this will not deter him or his efforts. He is aware of what you have accomplished so far and continues to have faith that you will succeed. Go now and return to the castle; lay your plans carefully and have an alternative ready, should things not transpire too well."

Matt and James mounted their horses and left Aragon behind them as they made their return. Both said little but thought hard trying to consider everything before making a plan. The others would need to play a part and James gave up after a short while suggesting that they waited until they could all put their heads together.

The next morning the boys went to the stables early and sought out their respected, though temporary, squires. There was little movement or sound from anywhere since most of the stables carried competitors horses that had already been eliminated from the competition. James wasn't going to take the chance of being overheard though and led the horses and his team out of the castle.

He didn't travel far, he didn't need to. He didn't want to practise this time he just wanted to be sure that they could all speak privately. They dropped below an incline that took them out of view of the castle and they sat down together.

"Right, this is the plan as I see it, but, it is by no means set in stone and I am open to ideas and tactics that we could employ to make it better.

"Both Matt and I will lose our respected jousts today which will give us a reason for not going to the banquet tonight. The two remaining competitors, apart from us, are Sir Thomayne's men. Matt and I will make sure that each run is tied then the decision for the victor must be made by Thomayne himself. He is sure to choose his own man which will give us an opportunity to show displeasure at his decision and refuse to go to the banquet tonight.

William and Richard will prepare the horses for travel; leave behind anything we do not need."

"What about the archery and sword events?" William asked.

"Both Matt and I will do our very best to win the finals today, it has proved beneficial that they should fall a day before the jousting final. The purse we receive for them, I will give to you William to secure three more horses so that we can ride hard when we leave."

"There should be some for sale here somewhere, don't worry, leave it to me, I won't let you down, "William replied.

"Whilst you are tending to that, and when the feasting starts, Mary will show us the way down to where the sword is kept. The rest is simple, bring the sword back here, collect our mounts and get out of here as fast as we can. When we are in range of Merlin, he will find us and take the sword back to Camelot and its rightful owner."

"It all sounds so simple, too simple," Richard pointed out.

"The beauty of simple plans is that there is less to go wrong," Matt argued.

"I suppose, but the risks we are taking. We will be tortured and killed if we are caught."

"We'd better make sure that we aren't then. Now we had better get back for we have some events to prepare for."

The rest of the morning passed by quickly, both Matt and James practised their disciplines and then relaxed for the remaining time between lunch and the tournament.

Matt's sword final promised to be a fairly even contest. Both competitors had watched each other during the earlier rounds and knew each other's particular skills and slight weaknesses.

Sir Jeffrey was not one of the men who allied himself with Thomayne and was in the final on his own merit. He had been gracious in each of his earlier round victories congratulating his opponents for their skill and effort. This had made him quite a favourite with the crowd so Matt was viewed as a definite underdog to win.

As the two men entered the arena the crowd erupted into a huge cheer and different portions of them started to call out each of their names. They marched toward the centre and bowed graciously to their host and the evil Sargo who sat beside him and smiled her radiance for all to see.

The announcer introduced each of the knights to the crowd before and told them both to make sure that the fight would be conducted in the true spirit of knighthood. Both men nodded their agreement and then raised their swords and brought them together lightly in a mark of respect for each other and then they separated and took their places and waited for the signal to start.

The signal came and Matt and Sir Jeffrey approached each other sideways offering as small a target as they could for the first onslaught. Matt had already made up his mind to defend first and waited for Sir Jeffrey to launch his attack. He didn't have to wait long for suddenly, as fast as a striking viper, Jeffrey made his move. The speed of it surprised Matt but he parried the vertical blow from him and held his opponents sword easily above his head with his own.

"Your fast Sir Jeffrey but you are going to have to do better than that," Matt taunted using the same psychological tactics that he would with opponents on the rugby pitch.

"That was just a tester Sir Matthew and I promise there is much more to come," Sir Jeffrey responded and Matt found himself grinning inside his helmet.

Matt pushed Sir Jeffrey away and parted the still connected swords. Then he feigned an attack from the left, altering at the last second to come in from the right. The swords clashed as Sir Jeffrey matched his speed and guile and the crowd roared their approval. They traded blow after blow and tried all their skills to gain an advantage that could be pressed home and achieve victory but the two of them were equally matched in every department and the fight went on and on.

After twenty minutes the two of them were showing signs of tiring and the crowd knew that a victory was not that far away. Lifting the heavy swords was becoming increasingly hard work and Matt could feel the strength sapping away from him. His only comfort was the fact that he knew his opponent would be feeling the same.

Sir Jeffrey launched another attack and it was all that Matt could do to parry it and as he countered it immediately his right foot slipped in the dusty surface of the arena and he went down. The crowd gasped but that wasn't quite the end of it for as Matt fell he caught the back of Sir Jeffrey's knee and his leg collapsed underneath him. Sir Jeffrey was unable to prepare himself to break the fall and instead fell right on top of Matt with his sword pointing towards the underneath of

Matt's chin. There was nothing that Matt could do about it, the swords position automatically announced the victory for Sir Jeffrey. The crowd roared as their favourite managed to stand. He helped Matt to his feet and raised his own visor.

"That was misfortunate Sir Matthew and I take no pleasure from winning in that manner. That was one of the best fights I have ever had the fortune to partake in and I thank you for the heart you put into it. If you hadn't have slipped I am not sure that would have won."

Matt raised his own visor.

"It was unfortunate but sometimes things just happen. I promise you that I enjoyed that as much as you and I acknowledge your courage, strength and skill."

"As I do yours Sir Matthew."

The two men gripped forearms before moving toward Sir Thomayne and Sargo who still stood clapping in appreciation.

"Well fought Sir Knights, I would not be exaggerating if I said that it was one of the best fights I have ever seen. Bad luck cost you the victory Sir Matthew but I hope that you will both return next year and grace the arena with your swords again. Extend your sword Sir Jeffrey."

Sir Jeffrey extended his sword towards Sir Thomayne and he hung a leather pouch by a drawstring onto the tip of it.

"The winner's purse is yours Sir Jeffrey." He said before sitting down again.

Sargo smiled at both of them and sat down herself as Matt and Sir Jeffrey left the arena.

James came to meet Matt as he walked into the enclosure.

"Matt that was fantastic, you were fantastic, what a fight and what bad luck to lose in the manner you did or was that deliberate?"

"It wasn't deliberate, my foot just slipped. To be truthful I didn't have much left though so even if I hadn't have slipped I am not sure that I could have won that fight."

"He was in the same condition as you were Matt, from an observers position it was probably easier for me to see that then you. The result could have gone either way."

James and Richard helped him out of his armour and he sat down on a stool. His body shimmered with perspiration and droplets fell from everywhere.

"You look absolutely exhausted Matt."

"I am! The pressure is on you now James to win the archery. If we don't secure the prize money and get the horses then we are never going to put enough distance between us and this place."

"I have a good chance Matt, whilst my three opponents are worthy adversaries, I don't really think they are as good as I am especially over the longer distances. But don't worry; I am not taking victory as a foregone conclusion, I will be concentrating as hard as they will."

"I have every confidence in your ability with the bow James, I have seen you fire arrows before remember."

"I don't think I will ever forget that time against Robin Hood."

"Just think of this competition as being against him and you will win for sure."

Chapter 12: Bows and Arrows

The archery competition final was announced and the four men left to compete for it stepped into the arena. James was the only knight left in whilst the other three were in Sir Thomayne's growing army.

The army had been growing steadily for months but he paid for the loyalty his men portrayed and had to resort to ill-gotten gains to support the large wage bill. James led the small group out, as was his right as the only knight competing.

Like the two finalists in the sword fighting they marched to the centre of the arena where they bowed to Sir Thomayne and Sargo. Thomayne congratulated them all in reaching the final and endowed extra praise on his own three men. He waved the winner's purse in front of them to encourage them to aim and shoot true before wishing them all well.

There were four targets set across the arena at different intervals, thirty, fifty, seventy and one-hundred paces. The first two targets had three sections circled and the bull's eye was generous in size and relatively easy to hit. The third target had four circles with the centre being half the size of the first two, and the last had five circles with the centre being the same size as the third. The whole target was hard enough to hit from such a distance but to gain a bullseye would take considerable skill.

Each archer would have five arrows at the first two targets with the worst archer being eliminated at the end of the second set of targets. Another archer would be eliminated from the competition after the third round shoot leaving just two to compete on the last target.

Four sets of arrows lay on a small table each with a different colour feathering on the shafts. They drew lots for them and James drew the white set. He checked each arrow for straightness and was pleased with the quality of workmanship that had been used to make them.

Next they drew lots for the firing order and James set up in third position. It wouldn't matter after the first round because the worst performing archer would fire first and the others in order. The best was always left for last; it added to the pressure on the archer and kept the crowd interested until the very last arrow had been fired.

The crowd cheered as the competitors were told to take their positions for the first round. There was no clear favourite here. James had been careful not to display his full skill and bring unwanted attention to himself, although he had won his previous rounds he had always scored just enough to take the victory.

At thirty yards it was expected that all the archers would score bulls eyes with each arrow, they were after all bread and butter shots, and the competitors didn't disappoint. The order of firing on the fifty pace target remained the same.

The crowd were pleased with the closeness of the competition and wagers were being laid down amongst them. The silence was total as the first man fired his first arrow and then erupted as he hit the centre of the target. Each man scored three bulls and it was looking as if the next round might have four competitors instead of the allotted three, but on the fourth arrow the man firing second missed the centre by a few millimetres. His shoulders slumped visibly in disappointment as he moved back from the firing zone.

The crowd groaned with disappointment and sympathy towards the unfortunate archer. At the end of the second round he was the only competitor to have missed the centre and was eliminated to a generous cheer from them.

The third round carried forward the reputation of being the sorter. The distance was beyond the normal requirements for such accuracy and was guaranteed to present problems for the average archer.

James was firing second and waited patiently for his first turn. The first archer took aim and let loose his arrow which settled into the ring next to the centre. If the third target had been the same as the first two then it would have scored a bull but this was a smaller target. The crowd were generous with their applause, at this range it was a good shot.

James stepped forward and selected one of his arrows. He placed it against the bow and took a deep breath. What was it that Robin had told him all that time ago? Pull back on the string, raise the bow above release point, lower, taking aim and release as soon as possible. Don't hold it at full pull for a split second longer than you have to. Feel the shot. He smiled at the sudden memory and followed the advice of a man he had come to trust. The arrow flew straight and true and settled in the centre of the bull. The crowd roared with appreciation.

James did enough to win the round, but only just and another archer was eliminated.

The final target was so far away that the centre of it wasn't very clear. James squinted his eyes, almost shut, in an effort to gain a better focus. The target cleared and he could make it out.

As the winner of the last round he would be firing last and he knew that hitting the target at this range, with any real degree of accuracy and, with the primitive equipment he had, would be difficult.

His confidence grew and spread through his body as his opponent's first arrow whistled past the target missing it by a few centimetres. He took position and followed the technique he had used before. He let the arrow fly and watched it climb in the air before starting to dip and finally hitting the target just off centre.

Both men hit the target just off centre with the second and third arrows and then James' opponent scored higher than him with the fourth.

James still held the overall lead though and knew that all he had to do was hit the target one more time and victory would be his.

As he strode forward to take the firing position the crowd cheered sensing victory just a shot away and then as he selected his last arrow the arena grew so quiet that he nearly checked to see if they were still there. They remained as quiet whilst he took aim, whilst he fired and all through the flight of the arrow. Then as it landed in the centre of the bull the crowd erupted into cheers and James saluted them.

His opponent walked up to him and conceded gracefully, no longer needing to fire his last arrow. He simply couldn't score enough. Then the two of them gathered the two other opponents and they marched together toward Thomayne and Sargo.

It was Sargo herself who presented James with the winner's purse. She stepped down from the stand and stood in front of him holding him in a deep stare that he couldn't break away from.

"You're arrows fly straight and true Sir James; I trust that the journey you are on is as straight and true," She said quietly and gave him the smile that could delight a thousand men.

James felt a chill sweep through him. The message was barbed, she knew why he was here and what he was here to do, he was sure of it. Her witchcraft was strong, there could be no mistake, but he wondered if she knew anything beyond the basic facts, and even if she did it wouldn't deter him from his quest. There was too much at stake here, years of war, lives and suffering to prevent.

James knew that she, as his next adversary, was going to be tougher than the archer he had just competed with and that she wouldn't play by the rules. The plan he had formed was good, it was set for the right moment, of that he was sure, but the feeling of dread invaded his usual spirit and determination briefly before he shrugged it off. He knew that he couldn't and wouldn't back down.

He made his way back to the enclosure where Matt awaited his arrival. He slapped him on the back and congratulated him on his win before he noticed the worry etched in his friends face.

"What is it James, why so worried?"

James told him what had transpired in the brief moments that he had faced Sargo.

"She might suspect something James and was just testing you out."

"I don't think so Matt, the Witch knows why we are here. What I can't be certain of is how much she knows; if she is aware of our plans or not."

"Does it matter if she does or not? I mean we are not exactly going to change them are we?"

"We cannot, there is not enough time but I think we ought to voice our fears to Aragon and at least explain to him that we might need his services tonight."

"That makes sense but you need to do it now James the Jousting will start soon and we need to prepare for it."

James nodded. "Cover for me, I will go back to the stables and make contact with Aragon there. There is just too much noise here and I will need to concentrate. Get William and Richard to prepare the horses whilst I have gone, I shouldn't be too long."

"Richard and Mary went back to the stables to fetch some of the tack for the horses already so you might well see them there or pass them on your way."

"No worries, I'll send them back before I try to make contact with Aragon just in case he shows up."

By the time James returned, the horses had been prepared and all that was left to do was put on their armour. Neither of the boys enjoyed wearing the heavy metalwork. It was restricting and slowed them down despite needing its protection. They were fortunate in as much as they hadn't been drawn to joust each other and for the first time they were housed at the same end of the arena.

Remember James we need to draw this contest and be eliminated by Sir Thomayne decision and that will give us enough reason to show contempt and refuse to go to the finalists feast tonight."

"Don't worry Matt, I'll put on a little show of temper at the end of this that will not amuse anybody."

Matt grinned and slapped the rump of James, mount to encourage it to leave the enclosure. William took up position alongside James' horse carrying the lance. A mounted knight from the other end of the arena left his enclosure and rode towards him. When they met in the centre they nodded to each other before turning to Thomayne and Sargo and bowing politely. Then they retraced their paths to the start position.

The announcer called for their attention and explained the rules, rather unnecessarily considering they had been competing for the last few days, then told them to commence their first run at the drop of the cloth.

They charged the second the cloth touched the ground and both men drove their lances into their opponent's armour scoring a point each. They did this twice more and the joust was drawn three points each.

The competitors took position in front of Thomayne who looked at each without expression.

"Well fought Sir Knights." He said and the expectant crowd waited for his arm to rise in salute of his chosen winner.

He raised his left pointing to James opponent and James threw down his lance in apparent disgust, much to the crowd's disapproval who booed him.

"There was nothing to choose between us but I suppose it could only be expected that you would support one of your own Sir Thomayne."

A look of anger swept across Thomayne's face but James turned his mount away before he could answer.

Matt's joust went exactly as the boys had planned and he too expressed his displeasure in the same manner as James.

Chapter 13:
Thieves in the Night

Everything started to happen very quickly after that.

Richard went off to try and buy some extra horses whilst Mary started to gather their things ready for their departure later that evening.

Matt and James discussed their route into the dungeons with William and tried to organise a backup plan should anything go wrong. Despite their efforts, the simple truth was that there wasn't another plan to be had. There was only one route to the dungeons and they would have to take it. There were at least, several places to hide if somebody was to come their way but apart from that there were no alternatives to the main plan.

They did think about hiding the sword somewhere else but with Sargo and her Witchcraft it, was unlikely that she wouldn't be able to find it. Get it and flee was the only option.

Richard returned, just before they were due to set off, with three good looking mares to add to the pair they already had. Now at least they would all be able to ride at a fast place and increase the distance between them and Castle Witch.

Matt noticed that there were no saddles though, but when he mentioned it to Richard he told them that there was no need for them as he, William and Mary had all ridden bareback at times. They could never have afforded the luxuries of saddles.

Matt, James and Mary left Richard and William tending the horses and made their way to the same castle entrance that Mary had used before.

Before entering Matt sent her to make sure that Sargo and Thomayne were still present at their feast in the great hall. They were, and she returned undetected after only a couple of minutes had passed.

They slipped in through the entrance and crossed the ruined hall to the doorway on the other side. The boys felt more relieved when they reached the relative safety of the corridor. From here they knew they couldn't be seen and they held the advantage as they could hear anything approaching them from either direction. Sound travelled far down these narrow spaces and there would be more than adequate warning for them to hide behind one of the many doorways they passed.

They descended down deeper and deeper into the bowels of the castle without interruption and without making a sound themselves until Mary finally pointed to the door of the room that held the sword.

They listened carefully with their ears pressed firmly against the door before they became satisfied that nobody was in there. James lifted the latch and the door opened silently. There, as Mary had seen before, lay Excalibur on a cushion of soft material, glinting lively in the light of a single torch that lit the space. They crossed towards it and Matt picked it up.

Initially, he was surprised at how light it seemed compared to the weight of the sword he had used earlier that day. He looked carefully at it and felt the way it seemed balanced in his hand. Then he swung it above his head and swished it from side to side.

"Look what I have in my hand James, it's a piece of history, a legend in its own right."

James grinned, knowing exactly what his friend meant and took it from him and proceeded to copy Matt's example, cutting through the air with a few fast swipes.

"Ok, we have it, so now let's get the hec out of here." He said burying the sword into the scabbard at his side.

They left the room and started back; Mary pointing out the door of the Witch's lair.

"As much as I would like to take a peek in there we can't afford the time." James told her and continued walking back the way they had come.

They moved fast covering the distance almost twice as quick as the first time and soon mounted the stairs that led to the disused hallway. Carefully, Matt pushed the door open and peered around it. The hall was barren and he stepped out. As James followed him, a noise alerted them and they stopped instantly. They crouched down as if to hide, but there was nothing to hide behind. Then Thomayne entered the space form the other side along with six of his knights.

Mary, who had yet to come through the doorway, froze and James whispered some instructions to her. She disappeared along the corridor towards the great kitchen that she had seen before.

"So, what do we have here sneaking around the ruins like thieves in the night? Well, well! If it isn't Sir Matthew and Sir James," he said approaching them with his men fanning out ready to prevent a last minute escape from Matt or James.

"Thought it would be nice to visit parts of the ruins that are normally unseen by guests here. It's an amazing place have you explored it all yourself Sir Thomayne?"

"Spare me the lame rhetoric Sir Matthew I am fully aware of your purpose here and what you hope to accomplish. Unfortunately, you have been thwarted in your efforts and now will have to pay the ultimate price for your treasonous acts."

"You dare to lecture us about treacherous activities after what you have done at Camelot and at King Arthur's expense," James retorted angrily.

"Yes I dare, I dare because these are my lands and I am in charge and as such I can do anything I please. Now Sir James, you have something that belongs to me in your scabbard," he said holding out his hand to receive it.

"I have nothing of yours Thomayne for the sword belongs to another as you well know."

"Come, come Sir James surely you know of the legend that surrounds Excalibur. Only its true owner can wield it in a fight. If you had Excalibur there then you would not be able to swing it. The sword belongs to me and I would like it back now please."

Thomayne's men all drew their swords and James knew that he didn't have a choice. He drew the sword from its casing and laid it gently on the ground. The moment he straightened the knights surrounded them both and they were seized by the arms.

Thomayne picked up Excalibur and held it in front of his face examining it carefully as if to check for a scratch on the shiny metal work.

"Take them to the dungeons; I will deal with them later or perhaps Sargo would like to test some of her magic out on them; that would be worse than anything I could do to them and I know I would enjoy watching them suffer.

The two of them were led back down the route they had come from once again, temporarily stopping whilst Thomayne returned Excalibur to where they had taken it from. Then they were marched further down the long tunnel until it stopped suddenly at a pile of fallen rubble. A door on their right was opened and the knights pushed them through.

Inside, chains were attached to them at the wrists and the ankles and then shackled to huge rings set deep in the stone walls. They were left standing upright against them; the chains not long enough to allow them to sit.

"Enjoy your stay." Thomayne grinned as he said it and closed the door behind him leaving the two of them alone.

"Well, that didn't go too well then!" Matt said in a matter of fact way.

"No, it certainly didn't."

They looked around the space that confined them and saw that it was smaller than Excalibur's prison, probably only half the size.

The area was lit by a single flaming torch and they could see the edge of the drop off to their right. The height was sufficient enough to drown out all sounds of the sea from the base of the cliffs though and they could only estimate the true extent of the drop.

"Getting out of here is not really going to be such a problem for I am sure that Aragon could help us if we need him too but there is no telling what has happened to Richard, William and Mary. I only hope she got to them quickly enough to warn them to get out."

"Is that what you told her to do?" Matt asked.

"Yes, it was best for them and us. If they were captured too then they could be used as leverage against us, or they might simply be tortured to death or Sargo might inflict them with something Witchy. Yes it is better if they just flee the castle."

"Sounds to me like you have thought all this through so what are you suggesting we do?"

"For the moment nothing! I reckon that Thomayne will visit us later tonight after he has consumed vast amounts of alcohol. He won't be thinking at his best and I suspect that we might be used in some horrible way to amuse him. Or he might take us to Sargo's lair for her to do something to us. Either way I don't think it will be that pleasant. I am going to have Aragon standing by just in case we need him. He will be able to hide somewhere amongst the cliffs, on a ledge or in a cave or something."

"Didn't Merlin tell us that Aragon could revoke the Witch's powers by consuming her with flames at midnight?"

"He did but somehow I think tonight's celebrations will continue well past midnight so that opportunity won't arise. I would like to have kept Aragon's existence secret from her if possible so that we might get the chance to remove her magic at another time but if we are facing death from torture or Witchcraft we may have to reveal him sooner than I would have liked."

"Well let's just see what happens first although I don't think that being stuck in this position for hours is going to be very comfortable."

"I think I can help with that, one of my wrist bracelets is a little loose if I can undo it completely we can free our hands and at least sit down for a while."

"If you can do that then, shouldn't we escape?"

"The door is latched on the other side and I don't particularly fancy cliff climbing at night."

"Mmm! Sitting will be good then."

James freed his wrist and then unthreaded his other shackle. Reaching across he released Matt from one and waited whilst he released the other. The two of them sat down. There was little else to do and they passed the time recounting some of their other adventures through the portal. James' predictions proved accurate and it was several hours past midnight before the two of them heard approaching footsteps echoing along the tunnel.

They stood quickly attaching their shackles to their wrists and waited for the door to open.

Thomayne entered, clearly the worse for having drunk too much, followed by a much more calm and collected Sargo who smiled the most radiant of smiles again.

"I trust you've not been too uncomfortable," she said so sympathetically that they almost believed her.

She reached forwards and unscrewed a shackle on Matt's wrist"

"Free yourselves and sit down for there are things that we need to speak about."

They did as they were told before Matt asked her in his own direct fashion if she was about to place a spell on them or even kill them.

"I am sure that I have a better option for you than that, call it an opportunity to join forces with the winning side in a forthcoming battle."

Matt said no more and waited for her to explain herself further.

Chapter 14: Treachery

Matt and James waited patiently for her to continue speaking but instead she just looked at them and bestowed her most enchanting smile upon them.

They knew of course that this was her way and that the smile was sure to be a ruse to gain some sort of trust but they were immune to it. If anything it made them even more distrusting and positively uneasy. Still they waited; not returning the smile, making it seem like an unstipulated challenge until James finally broke the silence.

"Speak woman because frankly I haven't got all night to wait about whilst you display your pearly whites."

For a moment Sargo looked bemused at what James had said and the smile faded for an instant before she composed herself and it returned to its full radiance.

"For years now the people of this country have grown poorer under the rule of King Arthur. Whilst he languishes about at Camelot his people have fallen victim to famine and disease. It is time he is replaced with a King who truly values the common man and their value to the crown."

"By that I suppose you mean Sir Thomayne," James retorted angrily.

"Sir Thomayne cares about the common man and will take good care of them. He will lead this country well; as a leader in battle he will ride with the first offence. In domestic matters he will act as a fair and impartial judge and he will see an end to disease and famine."

"I don't actually think he will have too much to do about any of the things you have mentioned.

"The sword he stole from Camelot was only possible because of the way you manipulated its power and allowed any man to wield it. Before, it served as a symbol of power for Arthur but now it will be seen as something different for Thomayne for everybody will know that he stole it.

"The disease and famine are direct results of your Witchcraft and as far as being fair and impartial, well that just depends on what he has to gain," Matt said indignantly.

"You are most observant and mostly correct in what you've concluded except that a new legend will be created around Excalibur. The story will tell of how Thomayne won it in a head to head battle with Arthur shattering the belief that the sword has magical qualities."

"Since the sword has been out of Arthur's possession for some time now and the fact that everybody at Camelot and beyond is aware that it has been stolen, how do you propose to change the facts into a new story?" Matt pressed.

"Simple Witchcraft really; the same Witchcraft that grants me wisdom and knowledge that I continue to accumulate to serve my needs. The same Witchcraft that allowed me to see your journey here from Merlin's shelter in the woods and the same Witchcraft that tells me that you two are not really knights at all but just commoners. Oh yes! I know and see all Matthew and James and I can predict the future too, your future if you make the right decisions."

"You mean that we can have a very good future if we follow you and Thomayne," James responded quickly.

"Of course or, alternatively, you could have no future at all except a long fall to the sea below."

"We didn't exactly come here alone you know, we have friends of our own." Matt stated.

"True but the only true adversary that could have faced me and even give me a semblance of challenge would have been Merlin but he is held at bay by the strength of my own magic. And who else is there, surely you don't mean your squire William and his little daughter Mary, who even as we speak are being tortured for information. And then of course there is Richard, the other squire. He would sell his soul for money and a future and indeed that is what he did. How do you think we knew about your little plot earlier tonight? A little magic and a simple purse of money is all it took to persuade him to tell me everything."

Matt and James reeled inside at the news of Richard's treachery but managed to keep their faces impassive even when Sargo lifted her head back and laughed delightedly at what she knew they were thinking even if they didn't show it.

"We have more friends than those you have mentioned Sargo and some are more resistant than you think. Perhaps we could arrange a meeting between you and them. Say, about midnight tomorrow, how does that sound?" James asked candidly thinking of Aragon.

"I am not interested in any more of your pathetic friends but I am interested in Merlin and tomorrow you and I and a few friends of mine will ride hard to greet him."

"And if we refuse?"

"The girl Mary will die a very painful death and in front of her doting father. Now rest for what little of the night remains for we will be riding hard tomorrow."

Sargo left the dungeon chuckling to herself.

"Doesn't look like we are going to have much choice in the matter Matt," James said angrily.

"It's not such a bad deal really, William and Mary will be safe as long as we do as we are told and Sargo is taking a real chance leaving the sanctity of her realm and entering Merlin's. She must really fancy her chances against him."

"She has no knowledge of Aragon though and away from Castle Witch she is vulnerable to an attack from him."

"You are thinking a midnight attack here?"

"Oh, most definitely."

"Let's try and get some sleep there must be a couple of hours left, at least she didn't shackle us again."

"Not much point really was there, the only way out is straight down."

The two of them curled up on the floor and shut their eyes and found the blissful silence of peace whilst they slept. They woke as dawn's early light permeated the dungeon.

"That sleep was woefully short," Matt complained yawning and stretching at the same time.

"Long enough for now, I reckon our travelling partners will be arriving shortly considering the distance we are about to travel."

"It makes sense to leave early but even if we canter most of the way we are not going to be at Merlin's until darkness."

"I don't think they have any intention of seeing Merlin today, it's more likely they will confront him in the dawn of tomorrow, a surprise attack I would guess."

"I wonder if it would be possible to surprise Merlin at all, I mean he would expect something from Sargo to happen any time and has probably expected that for some time. No! Thinking about it I reckon he will be prepared for something out of the ordinary like this."

"I am going to contact Aragon and tell him what we know; he can warn Merlin for us which rather puts our worries about his safety to bed."

Footsteps echoed along the tunnel outside their prison, increasing in volume until they stopped outside the door. It opened and four men in full armour and with swords already in hand, entered and surrounded them. The leader spoke.

"Your presence is required outside," he said simply and prodded James with the tip of the sword.

James felt the slight sting of the sword, as it pierced his skin and shed a droplet of blood, and he followed two of them outside into the tunnel. Matt followed him after receiving a similar prompt and the two other armoured men brought up the rear. They were marched outside the castle where four more armoured men, Sargo and a string of saddled horses waited. There was no sign of Thomayne.

With a guard of eight fully armoured men there was no thought of escape, at least for the moment and

Matt and James mounted the horses that they were led to. Sargo led the column at a canter whilst Matt and James settled in mid position behind four soldiers and in front of four more.

For nearly six hours they rode unchecked, slowing to a walk when they faced an incline but otherwise maintaining the canter. The miles disappeared behind them fast and the boys started to believe that they might get to Merlin before it got dark but they had only passed this way once and at a completely different pace and neither could really estimate with any degree of confidence.

Just after noon they stopped for food and water at a stream and gave the horses a respite. Sargo joined Matt and James and sat beside them without invitation.

"If we maintain this speed you will see your old friend in the morning," she told them smiling fully.

Matt looked at her and didn't bother trying to hide his disgust of her. *Why does she think that smile is going to work on me and James*, he wondered ruefully?

"What are your plans regarding Merlin?" James asked her directly.

"I plan to enlist his help of course. Imagine the power of our combined magic. He will face a similar question to the one I gave you last night."

"Why would he want to join forces with you?"

"Why to avert his inevitable demise of course."

She continued smiling as she nibbled at some berries; the red juice that stained her teeth gave her the most ridiculous look and reminded Matt of one of his favourite vampire films.

They were on their way again soon and it wasn't long before James started to realise that they were closer to Merlin's shelter than he expected to be. He contacted Aragon mentally, who informed him that Merlin knew exactly where they were. By the time they decided to stop for the night Matt estimated that they were only a couple of miles from Merlin's position.

Their guards had said little all day and six of them settled down to sleep not long after dark. The other two stood guard. Sargo suggested that Matt and James slept too especially as they had gained so little the night before. The two of them lay back and closed their eyes but neither concentrated on going to sleep instead they were in a deep conversation with Aragon.

"You could relieve her of her powers at midnight tonight Aragon, you know, consume her with fire and all of that," Matt projected his thoughts.

Aragon's reply came back almost immediately and what he was told worried him.

"It may not be as simple as that. I am unaware at this stage of exactly how powerful I really am. I am far from fully grown and even though we possess powers from birth they are not as potent as when we are fully grown. Of course I will attempt the process tonight, the opportunity is too great to pass by but she is a powerful one and remember, that after I attempt this I will no longer have the element of surprise on my side, if I fail then she will know of my existence and plot to rid the world of me."

"You can count on me and James to help you, just say what you need us to do and we will do it."

"I have always known that I can rely on you two just as Merlin has but there is much at risk here and failure could mean a war to end wars. Rest for a while my friends and ready yourself for a midnight visit from Merlin and myself."

"Do you need us to take care of the guards?"
"No, Merlin will take care of them with a little magic.

Aragon broke the communication leaving both Matt and James happier at what was about to transpire in a few hours' time.

Chapter 15: Aragon Attack

For the next few hours James and Matt got some well-earned rest before they were woken by the sound of Aragon's voice in their head.

"Be prepared for a visit from the one who sees all and don't worry about the guards, they have all been taken care of already."

Immediately, they sat up and looked around them. The soldiers looked as if they were just asleep but they couldn't see the two patrolling guards. Sargo looked up at their sudden movements and smiled her accustomed smile that had a luminescent quality about it in the glow from the camp fire.

"Finding it difficult to sleep with the impending attack on Merlin just a few hours away?"

"Lack of sleep has nothing to do with worrying about Merlin, it is more the expectation that you will be rewarded in a way that you might not expect when you finally meet him," James answered giving her his best imitation of her smile.

Matt stifled a laugh at his friend's toothy reply and sat quietly listening for a sound that would betray Merlin or Aragon's arrival but he could hear nothing.

Sargo looked surprised at James' response but said nothing further and instead watched them intently making them feel uneasy. They were careful not to show it though and the fact that her stares had no apparent effect on them irritated her. She stood up and walked around the camp fire making a show of warming herself which was a little silly considering it was a very mild night.

"It looks to me as if you are the one that feels uneasy, if you ask me. I'm not surprised, and you should be. Merlin is no easy opponent to take on and you are in his domain area. You're magic isn't as strong here as it is at Castle Witch is it?" Matt taunted.

"Be quiet man or I will show you just how effective my magic is by sealing your mouth shut," Sargo snapped and the smile disappeared from her face.

Matt raised his eyebrows at James who winked a reply back. She was worried, far more than she had been showing.

Then from nowhere Merlin appeared, suddenly and silently standing directly in front of her. At first, and for a brief second, she did not notice him as her focus lay in the embers of the fire. Then she was unable to prevent herself from jumping at the sight of the wizened old man who stood before her.

"You! You came to me!" she exclaimed trying to hide her shock.

"Why does that surprise you Sargo, surely you didn't expect me to wait for you to ambush me in the morning."

"How do you know about that?"

"I know about a lot of things, far more than you think. For example I know of your plans for the kingdom and for Arthur. I know about your plans for Matt and James here and Richard, William and Mary. I know of all that you have plotted with Thomayne, all of your evil treachery. Surely you didn't think otherwise did you?"

"Your powers are legendary Merlin but my own have grown to a level that is more than a match for you."

"Sadly, you are mistaken and I mean sadly too for we could have secured a power stronger than anything before us if we had been able to join forces and use it for the good of mankind."

"You'll forgive me if I tell you that I have other ideas on how to use my powers. Guards awaken," she commanded but they didn't even stir.

"Guards," she cried out again but the response was the same.

"I took care of your guards shortly after they fell asleep, a thunderstorm would fail to wake them at the moment. So you see for the meantime you are all alone Sargo."

"Well since these two are irrelevant," she said pointing at Matt and James, "it's just me and you then, my magic against yours."

"Alas, if only things were just that simple."

"Oh, but they are Merlin," and she finished the sentence with what sounded like a lot of nonsense.

From nowhere a vicious and violent whirlwind surrounded Merlin's body lifting him upwards into its swirling vortex. Merlin thrust out his staff but the words he spoke were lost in the sound of the wind. Almost as he finished the sentence the wind subsided and allowed his body to lower gently until his feet touched the ground once more.

"Is that the best you can do Sargo?" Merlin asked his face expressionless.

"Try this old man," She snapped and spouted more chants that sounded more like the language that small children use before they learn to talk properly.

This time lightning hit the ground close to Merlin's position but instead of moving and taking shelter from it Merlin raised his staff again and caught the next strike on the tip of it. The force ran down the staff and engulfed him and Merlin allowed it to wrap around his body. Then with direction and intent he forced his free hand forward and the force left him and struck a tree in the distance splitting it in half.

Still expressionless he looked directly into Sargo's eyes.

"Read what intent I have in my mind for you Sargo, see for the first time what power I intend to unleash onto you."

Merlin held her eyes locking them onto his own so that she was unable to break the stare. Then he forced the image of a dragon into her mind and could sense her fear.

"You cannot scare me with that Merlin everybody knows that dragons are no more."

"If that is so Sargo what is it that sits in the tree above you about to engulf you in fire and release you from your powers?"

Despite believing what she did, she could not resist looking upward and screamed as she registered what was there. A stream of fire erupted from Aragon's nostrils and engulfed her entire body.

Aragon held the flames on her for as long as he could before he released her and she slumped to the ground.

Matt and James were suddenly spurred into action themselves now that the captivating events had ceased. They stood and went to Sargo's prone body and rolled her over.

"She is not even charred let alone burnt Merlin, how can this be so?" James asked.

"The fire only consumes the magic, if there was no magic then the fire would have burned the body," Merlin replied.

"Has she lost all of her powers now?"

"Yes Matt, at least for a while. She was a strong Witch, a very strong Witch and Aragon is such a young dragon. He may well have to bathe her in his fiery breath again in the future. At least for now, she is powerless to prevent what we must do next. Excalibur must be returned before the next meeting at the round table or King Arthur may find trouble closer to home than Castle Witch."

"Surely, with your magical powers Merlin the rest should be easy."

"Not necessarily, the powers that Sargo used at Castle Witch may still be present. As it was her stronghold, spells that she cast there would be there still, unhindered by the loss of her power.

"We could leave her here, not take her with us."

"No, everyone must see what she has become without her power, by early morning her appearance will have altered and her true looks and age will be apparent. That in itself will serve as a deterrent to some that oppose Arthur.

Once seen in her more natural state, they will be aware that my powers were greater than hers. But that is not the case for those that she cast a spell on directly, they will continue as they have from the moment they came under her influence. The only thing that can cure them from the spell is the dragon fire or release by Sargo. Sargo can no longer do that and Aragon may not have the control needed over his power to use on a mortal without serious risk of harm."

Merlin prevented any further conversation by instructing them to sleep in preparation for another day's hard ride and the boys followed his instructions. Sargo lay quite close to them with her eyes closed to and Matt wondered if she was asleep, unconscious or under the magic of Merlin.

In the morning they rose early and they were horrified at the physical condition of Sargo. Her once serene face had sagged into what could only be described as layers of folded skin with deep chiselled lines separating them. The body, once young and supple had also lost its shape and form and she hunched at the shoulders. She looked over a hundred years old.

Merlin, told the boys to saddle up. Sargo and the soldiers remained in their sleeping positions. Aragon had disappeared from the tree and was nowhere to be seen.

"What about Sargo Merlin," James asked.

"She stays hereunder the spell of sleep."

They rode in silence and Merlin made no attempt to share his plans for the immediate future. This particularly frustrated Matt who asked the question the moment they stopped at a stream for fresh water.

"At this point in time I am unable to plan too much in advance until I know the extent of Sargo's Witchcraft I have to face."

"Surely that is weakened Merlin isn't it. I mean you are travelling beyond the point where her magic stopped you before."

"That is true Matthew but it is the powers over others that I am not sure about. For example Thomayne is definitely under a spell; I have no doubt that there will be others in important positions that are under her influence too. Richard will be as well, the man would not have betrayed you under normal circumstances."

"There might not be a plan at the moment but our objective remains the same surely, and that is to get Excalibur," James suggested.

"That is not enough now, we must release those under spells or they will attempt this all over again."

"Can you release them from Sargo's influence?"

"If I can't James then at least I will be able to deflect the magic in some fashion, change the focus of it and thus weaken it but I will know more when I meet each of the individuals affected."

"What will you require of Matt and I Merlin?"

"Might be very little, might be a lot but there will still be dangers to face and an enemy under a Witches control is a daunting prospect for any mortal being."

"I think one of the first things I want to do is to release Mary and William. I hate to think of either of them being subjected to torture and if they are still unharmed they could be of real assistance to us."

"You are right of course to think of their safety and well-being first and although Richard betrayed you, he too could be of great help in our quest if I can release him of the spell that holds him."

"It will be time to discard the horses soon for when we enter the castle I want us to enter as poor folk who represent no threat to anybody. From there we will attempt to rescue our friends and then hide in order to assess the opportunities that either fall to us naturally or those that we can make ourselves."

"I thought you said that you didn't have a plan Merlin, if that wasn't, then my name isn't Matthew."

"Let's just say that it is the starting point of my plans." Merlin answered trying to grin at Matt but appearing to sneer in his attempt.

Chapter 16: Free the Innocent

Before entering the castle Matt and James tore their clothing and dirtied it with some mud. They concealed their faces under the hoods of their cloaks for the last hundred yards or so and passed under the raised portcullis. Merlin had no need to follow their example for his clothing was already tattered but he did cloak his face to hide the unmistakable hair and wizened face.

Once in the castle ground they entered an empty stable and with a wave of his staff and a few unrepeatable words Merlin cast a spell over their temporary domain.

"What did you just do Merlin?" Matt asked curiously.

"I have secured this place for our use only. We are the only ones who can see and use the entrance.

From everybody else's perspective the lack of doorway means that this particular space doesn't exist; the only thing that you do need to be careful about is not to be seen apparently disappearing through walls."

"Cool Merlin, having somewhere where we don't have to fear capture is great," Matt responded.

"The first thing I need you to do is to find out where our three friends are."

"Can't you use your magic for that?" James asked. "I mean you knew all about Sargo's plans didn't you?"

"To be honest James I am not exactly a mind reader. The information I had learned about her came mostly from the careful and covert observations of Aragon."

"Matt and I will go and get the information we need, you just wait here, plot and scheme and come up with some plans for getting Excalibur back."

"Take these coins James and buy us some bread or something, it is easier to strike up a conversation with somebody when you are buying something from them."

Matt took the coins and the two of them went outside leaving Merlin alone with his thoughts. It didn't take long to find somebody selling food and they flattered the man's ego and bought food before striking up a conversation about the traitors who stole the Sword from the castle.

The man was as happy to talk as he was about to relieve them of the coins that Merlin had given them and they found out what they needed to know. They returned to Merlin with the news.

"What have you found out my friends?" Merlin asked.

"Richard has been rewarded for his services with a job as chief blacksmith of Castle Witch. He is in sole charge of developing stronger armour and weapons for Sir Thomayne's army who will ride to Camelot to contest the throne in a few weeks."

"We must stop this Matt, Richard is a very good blacksmith and he mustn't be allowed to succeed at his task and give Thomayne's army an advantage. It is clear that he is still under the spell of the Witch if this is the path he is on, for he would not have done this freely."

"What do you suggest; can you lift the spell he is under?" Matt persisted.

"Probably not, at least not whilst he remains in Castle Witch, but if I cast a second spell to reduce his ability as a smith then perhaps that would at least buy us some time."

"It will probably get him into more trouble and anyway there isn't really that much time because when Sargo doesn't return they will start searching everywhere for her, including this castle," James said, his voice etched with concern.

"That is the least of our troubles; a search for Sargo will reduce the size of our enemy in the castle and offer us opportunities to rescue our friends and get the sword. In any case they won't find her easily.

"I couldn't take the risk of bringing her here for she might regain her strength and magic once in her own territory. Now tell me about William and Mary."

"They are being kept in the dungeons close to where the trader believes the sword is kept. He heard that William has been tortured by Thomayne but so far Mary had been spared that and remains unharmed."

"If that is the case then we should do something about them quickly before he suffers anymore," Matt said emphatically."

"I agree but it would be pointless trying to rescue them and not going for the sword at the same time. My concern is that we don't know how bad a condition William might be in and this could hamper our retreat from the dungeons and the castle itself."

"Magic might help Merlin."

"Oh I can place a spell on him so that he feels no pain but what further damage might be done moving around on his injuries that he can't feel. I would only do that as a last resort."

"Can you not just heal him?"

"As far as I am aware there is no magic in existence that can cure damage to an injured body. Pain relief I can do but the body has to heal itself in its own way and time."

"So do you have a plan then Merlin?"

"As a matter of fact I do, or at least the start of one."

Merlin produced the grimace on his face that the boys had accepted as a smile before he spoke and kept them waiting, building the anticipation like a master story teller before he spoke again.

"I liked the plan that you had before, the one you used to retrieve the sword before you were betrayed but it is my guess that the tunnel of dungeons is guarded now and probably heavily. It worked before and it will work again but we just need to reduce the odds and swing them into our favour."

"What do you suggest then," Matt asked impatiently when Merlin paused for just a little too long for his liking.

"I want you two to go out again and start spreading the news that Sargo has been captured by Merlin who is holding her two day's ride from here. You can give them false directions if you like; tell them it is north of here.

"Within a couple of days things will happen, Thomayne will not be able to ignore her disappearance and send a force to find her, he will probably go himself and my guess is that the force will be considerable; she is just too important for his plans to ignore.

"When they leave we will make our move and I feel certain that any guards that stand in our way in the tunnels will have been reduced to cover the castle watch."

"It would be best if we went in the dead of the night when everybody will be in the deepest of sleeps Merlin," James suggested.

"You are correct, it will be the best time, now go and spread the rumours for it will take a little time before Thomayne decides to act."

Two days passed before the inevitable happened and Thomayne led a small army out of the castle in search of Sargo. James watched them go with satisfaction as they took a northerly direction.

Merlin was pleased with the outcome too, estimating that nearly half of Thomayne's forces had left the castle. It was an absurd amount of men to send for just one Witch but Thomayne would use any opportunity to demonstrate the power at his disposal.

James and Matt waited the day out impatiently prowling around the stable like two angry bulls in a ring. Merlin sent them out frequently on false errands that kept them busy for a while whilst he himself sat in quiet contemplation, statuesque like and so quiet that a sparrow landed on his shoulder and edged along it before flying off.

As evening fell, Merlin told the boys to rest and helped them achieve some sleep with a little magic before he woke them a few hours from dawn.

The three of them headed off towards the ruined hall that held the entrance to the corridor and tunnels that led to their prize. They moved silently past the stables and followed the wall along towards the blacksmiths workshop. The fire glowed brightly here and Richard's prone position on some straw at the back of the area showed that he was fast asleep. Merlin waved his staff and said a few incomprehensible words as they passed by.

"He will sleep until I wake him," Merlin whispered continuing forward.

Apart from the occasional hoot from an owl the castle was in complete silence and as they entered the ruined hall they spotted a guard at the entrance to the corridor. They approached him stealthily, scarcely breathing, uncertain whether he was awake or not. Luck was on their side and Merlin placed the same spell on him as he had on Richard. Then it was into the corridor, down the stone stairs and along the tunnel.

There were more torches emitting light in the dungeon tunnel than before and this forewarned them that its use had been increased. It also raised the certainty that there would be guards present, probably outside William's prison and possibly outside the swords home.

As they approached the final bend in the tunnel, which would reveal both dungeon doors, they came to a stop.

Merlin raised his staff and indicated for the boys to wait before rounding the bend. They waited for what seemed an eternity before Merlin returned and told them that both guards were sleeping peacefully.

They moved quickly now, knowing that their path was clear, until they stood beside the door that they believed held William and Mary.

The wooden bar that held it shut fitted tightly and Merlin struggled to lift it from the grip of the clasps. Matt added his brawn to Merlin's effort and it released suddenly causing Merlin to lose his balance in the sudden upward thrust. James grabbed at the man's shoulders and steadied him and Merlin grunted his thanks. Then the old man pushed the door forward and walked inside.

William and Mary were asleep on a carpet of straw. They were not tethered in any manner because there was no way that they could have escaped.

William's robe had been torn across the back and it was clear that he had been whipped and whipped badly.

James laid a hand gently on his shoulder and shook him. The man opened his eyes and fought to get a grip with what he was seeing.

"I didn't think I would ever see you two again," he said and tried to grin and sit up.

"As if we would leave you here to suffer goodness knows what, we came as soon as we could," James told him.

"Who is your friend?" William asked.

"This is Merlin."

"The magician?"

"The one and only, and he is here to help us get you out of here. How badly injured are you?"

"I have been beaten and stretched on the rack. I am in poor shape but my spirit is not lacking."

Merlin moved forward and examined William carefully.

"I can ease your pain but cannot heal your wounds. I do not believe that you will suffer any ill effect from a little magic."

"Pain relief would be very helpful as I have had little respite from it for a while now."

Merlin waved his staff and said something and William stood.

"That is amazing you truly are what the legends say you are Merlin."

Merlin acknowledged the thanks hidden in William's comments and asked after Mary.

"So far she remains unhurt but that is due to change upon Thomayne's return," William told him.

"Wake her quickly, we must get to the sword and relieve this place of its stolen gains," Merlin commanded.

William did as he was asked and they all left for the sword room. Thanks to Merlin's magic he moved as freely as he would have before he'd been tortured.

Chapter 17: Excalibur and Spells

Two doors further down the tunnel, the second guard sat slumped in the deep sleep that Merlin had placed him in.

James opened the door to see the sword lying in exactly the same place as it had been the first time they seen it. Matt went to pick it up but was unable to move it.

"What the hec! I can't lift it. It's almost as if it has been super-glued," he said in frustration.

James shot him a look as if to say be careful of what you say and Matt immediately realised he had mentioned something that Merlin could have no knowledge of.

"That's curious; it would seem as if Sargo's hold on the sword has been lifted and once again the only man to be able to move it would be King Arthur. I wonder!"

"I wonder what! If we can't move it we cannot return it," Matt said quickly.

"I believe Sargo's hold on it has been released because the sword does not come from here.

"Her hold on Richard and Thomayne and his men is still present; their absence tells us that.

"The magic she weaved on Excalibur before was powerful, probably more powerful than the average Witch could perform. It stands to reason that when Aragon removed her powers she was unable to keep a hold upon it and that leaves us with a problem of our own."

"Can't you place a spell on it of your own Merlin?"

"I have no doubt that I can but it wouldn't be with a shake of my staff and a few select words. The magic required would need to be more powerful than that and require preparation time."

"Are we talking hours or days Merlin?" James asked.

"More than just hours and I would need to collect a few things. I am afraid that we are not going to be able to remove it from the castle today."

"What if we were able to move it from here but not necessarily from the castle? Could you accomplish that?"

"Merlin thought for a moment.

"Perhaps that would be possible but I would need to increase my power to do it."

"What about Aragon, he told us that he had powers of his own could you not combine yours and his to move it just a little way?" James asked the beginnings of an idea forming in his mind.

"Where were you thinking of moving it too James?" Matt asked interrupting Merlin as he was about to speak.

"The stable of course, the very place where we have been hiding."

"Aragon could assist me with a spell to help you lift the sword and take it a short distance but I must warn you that there is a limit to his powers; he is such a young dragon. We would have to move fast before he weakens and the spell fades."

"Call him Merlin, do it quickly before dawn breaks. Matt and I will get it to the stable."

"Compared to how much we would run in a rugby match this is a stroll in the park and the distance is just within the range of sprinting," Matt said whispering to James.

They heard the whoosh of powerful wings and looked up to see Aragon at the open cliff edge of the dungeon.

"Merlin if you can do this then James and I will split the running distance. If James leaves now and waits in the ruined hall, I can sprint with the sword to him and then he can sprint to the stable."

"We can cast the spell and you will be able to move the sword but it will not be for long. As the spell weakens the sword will get heavier and heavier. If you make it James it will not be without the need of great strength as well as speed."

"Maybe we should change places James after all I am the strongest," Matt suggested.

"That is true but I am faster and that little extra speed could make all the difference," James responded and for once refusing to allow Matt to take the leading role.

"No James, I will go first, it's the right thing to do. Use your speed at the end when the sword is at its heaviest."

"Ok, but I think also that William could be of help in the last few paces to the stable," James added and for once he seemed annoyed by Matts argument even though he knew it was right.

"When Aragon and I have finished the spell we will be extremely weak and vulnerable. Aragon will have to stay here for a few hours to regain the strength needed to fly to safety and I will be the epitome of an old man who has lived for too long. I may not be able to get myself out of these tunnels."

"When I have passed over the sword to James I will return for you Merlin and we will leave together," Matt told him.

"And I will be grateful for your assistance. It is time for William, Mary and James to go, leave now and be swift in your travels. Aragon and I will start the spell after the count of one-hundred."

The talking stopped and Merlin started to count. James waited until the first few numbers had been said and he had picked up the rhythm of the count before ushering Mary and William out and starting to run.

Matt found the count frustratingly slow and paced the limited space of the dungeon under the curious eye of Aragon that seemed to follow him despite not moving.

James reached his spot after the count of seventy-five and explained where he wanted William to wait further towards the stable.

Finally, Merlin reached one-hundred and moved across to Aragon. He placed his hand on Aragon's folded-back wing and started to recite some words of a strange language that, although unknown or understandable to Matt, were sort of familiar, in as much as he had heard Merlin talk like this several times now.

A few seconds past and then Merlin pointed his staff at Excalibur. The staff began to glow, as if charging, before emitting a sudden burst of energy across the space between it and the sword.

"Now Matt!" Merlin called and Matt picked up the sword as if it was made of paper.

The energy stream disappeared and Matt sprinted away along the tunnel, up the stone stairs and beyond getting nearer to his friend by the second. As he neared he felt the weight of the sword increase slightly and called out to James.

"The spell is weakening already."

James grabbed it from him and Matt slowed to a gentle jogging pace fighting to get control of his breathing.

The weight of the sword increased with every pace now and as James passed the mark where he felt that he had travelled approximately three-quarters of his run, William stepped out from the shadows.

He could see that James was struggling and clasped his hands around the end of the sword blade and lifted. James felt immediate relief as the weight was shared but William felt the edge of the sword cut into his hand. He gritted his teeth and tried his best to match James' pace.

They approached the stable entrance severely stooped under the now immense weight of the sword and William dropped his end to open the door. James stopped dead unable to move it on his own and then felt William's hands around his waist trying to pull him through the door. They pulled and pulled to no avail and then in a blur, something hit James full in the stomach area. The strength of the hit created the force to drag the sword in and James fell backwards on top of the unfortunate William.

The pair of them wheezed painfully as they struggled to get enough oxygen to satisfy their bodies. Mary looked at them and laughed.

"Two grown men reduced to a tangled mess by the force of a humble child," she said and laughed in delight at the carnage she had caused by her charge.

"Mary, you have, saved, the day," William told his daughter proudly between gasps for air.

James managed to stand up and reach to where the sword laid. Stubbornly, it refused to move and James knew they had made it by the narrowest of margins.

Back along the tunnel Matt felt mortified as he saw the weakened state of Aragon and Merlin. Aragon was now lying down, devoid of any strength whilst it was all Merlin could do to stand himself up. He heard Aragon's voice in his head.

"You must leave me here and get out of this place Matt. I will recover after a little rest and leave when I am ready. Make sure that you seal the door as it was when you arrived so that if the guard wakes he will suspect nothing."

Matt could feel the tiredness in the voice and didn't argue. He placed one of Merlin's arms over his shoulder and semi dragged him from the cave. He stopped to secure the door and then started along the tunnel.

"I am unable to continue like this Matt you must leave me here and go and get help."

"I just need to carry you in a different way Merlin and I have a little magic of my own called a fireman's lift."

Merlin seemed a little bemused by this and then a little shocked as Matt lifted him and spread his weight along his shoulders.

"Tuck your head and feet in as best as you can Merlin, I don't want you hitting the tunnel walls and hurting yourself," Matt told him as he started to move off more quickly now.

Long after his strength was depleted, determination and will power kept him going, and he managed to reach the ruined hall and felt the freshness of the night air cool his perspiring brow. Despite this, he knew he had to stop and rest. Gently, he lowered Merlin down into a seating position and sat beside him.

"You and your friend have iron in your blood and compassion in your hearts and I am proud of what we have accomplished so far but you should get help; you are exhausted as I suspect your friends are too."

"There is little time for that Merlin the early light is starting to show on the horizon and people will soon emerge from their sleep. We will rest for another minute and then I will carry you once more. We started this together and we will finish this together," Matt told him remembering the favourite saying from the half-time talks his rugby coach used to make.

"That's right, Matt and that's the way it will always be." Another voice said and Matt looked up to see his best friend and William there to help."

"The sword?" Merlin asked.

"Safe and sound thanks to Mary," James said generously.

William and James reached down and helped Merlin to his feet.

"Piggy back relay all the way back to the stable." James announced and lifted Merlin onto his back.

Merlin and William looked bemused at James' language but Matt understood.

They reached the stable without being seen just as the first rays of the sun started to appear on the distant horizon.

Inside, and for the moment safe and sound, they slept and rested to ready themselves for the next stage; getting the sword out of the castle and preferably before Thomayne and his army returned, would still not be easy.

They must know by now, that Sargo had not travelled north and would search the west next, the very direction they needed to escape to. Thomayne might try south but only if they had no luck in the west.

When Aragon was rested and sufficiently strong enough to leave, Merlin asked him to track down Thomayne so that they could use avoidance tactics when they left.

Chapter 18:
Escape from Castle Witch

Huddled in the stable, the group sat and contemplated their next move. Merlin ordered Matt and James to rest as they had been awake more than twenty-four hours and were completely exhausted. They had refused since there was so much left to accomplish so Merlin gave them a weird tasting concoction, the ingredients of which were completely unrecognisable, but it refreshed them as efficiently as if they had just slept for the night.

"We need to leave this place as soon as possible Merlin, before the army returns and before they are close enough to cut off our escape route," Matt told him earnestly.

"We also need to retrieve Richard too. I can't leave my cousin here despite his betrayal," William added.

"Your cousin did not betray us of his own free will, I am sure of that William, and we will not be leaving without him despite the fact that he thinks otherwise at the moment."

William nodded his thanks to Merlin.

"The sword will have to stay here, there is no way we are going to be able to move it without remaining here longer whilst Merlin makes the magic he needs to counteract Sargo's," James said.

"The sword is not a worry at this time James for I can conceal it under a veil of magic that even Sargo couldn't have uncovered. It can remain in this very spot completely safe.

"The way I see things is that our first two objectives have already been stated; we must get Richard and get out of here. Aragon will oversee our route for us and we will journey to Camelot and reveal the swords location to Arthur.

"I am convinced he will send an army to Castle Witch, the size of which will deter Thomayne from offering resistance. The only problem I foresee is that Thomayne may still be under Sargo's influence and I have no idea how strong an influence that still is."

"We need to go under the cover of darkness Merlin; it will be easier to avoid Thomayne and it will help conceal us in the openness of the countryside around here."

"You are thinking about tonight then James?"

"Yes."

"If that is the case then I need to visit Richard to assess the power of the hold on him."

"He will recognise you Merlin and sound an alarm."

"He will not recognise me for he will not be able to see me, nor will anybody else."

"You can do that?"

"I can."

"Cool."

Merlin left their sanctuary and made for the blacksmiths workshop.

It was a while before he returned and he carried a small bundle under his arm. He handed it to Mary who took it and began to eagerly uncover the contents. Her face showed approval in the form of a smile as she revealed a large and, somewhat ungainly, looking loaf of bread. James looked at it with interest and thought of it as a slab of bread rather than a loaf. She shared it round and they all ate hungrily.

"What news of my cousin Merlin," William asked.

"He works like a possessed demon in the pursuit of making the finest swords in the land. He is, of course still possessed but not by a demon. Sargo's hold on him is strong; I can release him from it but not before spending time preparing; time we can ill afford at the moment. The magic will reduce in power as we move away from the castle but it will always be there until I remove it properly. I am thinking that that if we try to force him to come with us tonight we will be taking a huge risk. He could betray our presence or at the very least slow us down. I have another idea though."

"What is it Merlin?" William asked worriedly.

"Simple really; I propose to leave him here, where he is at least safe, and have Aragon bring him to us when we are safe and far from here."

William looked disappointed with Merlin's idea but appreciated the reasoning behind it. He nodded his understanding forlornly.

The rest of the day passed frustratingly slowly whilst they remained in their stables like prisoners awaiting release at the end of serving time.

As soon as it was dark they left and made their way to the portcullis where they knew they would have to face the guards who could potentially recognise them, especially Matt and James who had fared so well in the tournaments.

As they approached, Merlin stretched out his arm to signal them to stop whilst he alone moved forward to face the two guards.

"Where are you going old man?" One challenged.

"I'm travelling to see an old friend," Merlin offered.

"It would be wiser and safer to travel by the light of the day," The other said holding a torch up to illuminate Merlin's face properly.

"I have no choice but to leave now for my friend's needs are urgent. You will let me pass and forget that you have seen me or my party," He commanded waving his staff toward them.

The two turned their backs and walked back to their posts whilst Merlin signalled the others to continue and they all passed through the portcullis.

From there they travelled through the night at a steady pace before a swoop of large wings heralded the arrival of Aragon, who landed just in front of them and halted their journey.

Merlin told them all to take a brief break whilst he spoke to Aragon. The break stretched on for fifteen minutes or so before the beating of wings announced Aragon's departure and Merlin walked back towards them.

Matt looked at Merlin quizzically.

"Thomayne's army are but a few miles from here. He has searched the north and is in the process of doing the same with the west. We are unlikely to be able to avoid an encounter with some of his forces unless we can find a place to hide."

"Can you make us all invisible as you did yourself yesterday?" William asked.

"It will sap too much of my strength to do that with all of us and will endanger our chances of meeting Arthur."

"There is a wooded area ahead of us that may offer us some concealment; I can just make out the silhouette against the horizon," Matt suggested.

"Aragon also suggested this place Matt and he said it is the only area that we could hide in for several miles. It is likely that Thomayne has a patrol operating from his camp so we need to get there quickly to avoid any confrontation."

The group travelled quickly to the woods and were fortunate to miss the patrol, which Merlin had thought might be operating, by a few minutes. Of course they would be back though as the sweeps they made would continue throughout the night.

Moving towards the centre of the woods Matt discovered a bush that stretched for several metres and circumvented a few saplings. At first it looked impenetrable but Mary discovered a small gap, low down towards the ground, and she squeezed through on her tummy.

"Come and see this," she whispered excitedly. "There is enough room for us all in here although we will be unable to stand."

Matt crawled in and examined the space within. "She's right! This is as good a hiding place as we are likely to find anywhere."

The others crawled through and William cut a few branches above them so that they could at least sit comfortably.

"Now what?" He asked.

"Now we wait until the army move past us in the morning," James said thoughtfully.

"I think Thomayne will search these woods thoroughly because there is nowhere else nearby that Sargo could be hidden."

"I agree and if the need arrives I will aid our concealment with a little magic," Merlin added.

Thomayne and his army reached the woods just before midday and any hopes of not being discovered were dispelled when they heard the sound of hunting hounds.

"They have dogs, we are done for!" William cried in dismay.

"I can conceal us with magic but not for very long, possibly only long enough for the hunters to pass us by. It will be a very close thing," Merlin stated.

"What we need is a diversion, something to draw them away from here," James said emphatically.

"Whatever diversion we cause will surely get someone caught," Merlin replied.

"James and I used a tactic once before where we made out that the woods are haunted. A few select moans and wails, calls of pain and screams from an unseen source can unnerve the strongest characters and prove to be a powerful deterrent."

Merlin laughed delightedly. "I could call on Aragon's services as well; he has a call that could install fear in the wolves and bears."

"Can you magic me up a horse Merlin?" James asked determined to take the lead away from Matt.

"It will be of no real challenge but I am still glad we left the other horses behind though. We could never hide from anything with horses present. Look outside our hiding place."

There were two horses, beautiful black stallions complete with saddles idly standing there.

"Take them Sir Matthew and Sir James and play your tricks on our enemies then ride west for all you are worth until you reach Camelot and the King. Tell him what has gone on here and give him this."

He passed James a large twine threaded canine tooth the origins of which were unknown.

"Arthur will recognise this as mine and will know that you seek him under my instruction. Hopefully he will listen to what you say and ride towards us."

James took it and placed it around his own neck and tied the ends of the twine.

The boys said a brief farewell and headed off in opposite directions into the wood.

As Thomayne's soldiers and their dogs entered the trees they started their wails and moans. The seekers were instantly alarmed and became hesitant of entering the woods further than they had already. They waited, eyes wide opened and trembling before a final screech of such magnitude and dread inspiring force permeated the entire woods. Even Matt and James were startled and the hairs on their arms stood up before their rationality took over and they realised that Aragon had joined in.

Still in opposite directions, they left the concealment of the woods and rode as fast as their mounts could take them.

At first they hadn't considered their direction as they took flight but they hadn't gone far when James realised that he was heading East in the direction they had come from and slowly turned his mount until he faced the west and rode for Camelot.

Matt had left the woods at a slight angle and was heading northwest. As he rode he could see Thomayne's army to the right of him and angled away. The army saw him too and a group of eight soldiers broke away from their comrades and gave immediate chase.

James had a good head start though and managed to maintain a good distance between him and any possible pursuers. Slowly and almost imperceptibly, he turned until he was riding due west with only one thought on his mind; to reach Camelot.

He had not seen any sign of the enemy and continued at a more sedate pace trying not to exhaust his horse too quickly. He rounded a small incline in the terrain and was suddenly forced to rein up suddenly as he approached a group of four soldiers. He recognised one of the centrally positioned men in the group.

"Sir James how nice of you to join me once again!" Thomayne's voice emitted from the visor concealed face without trying to conceal the surprise at his sudden visitor's arrival.

Chapter 19:
A Fight to the Death

James was as surprised as Thomayne but soon realised that he had sent his army forward to conduct the search whilst he stayed in a place of relative safety.

"Perhaps Sir James you might join me in a little wine as I await my armies return for I am sure we have plenty to discuss," he said as two of his men moved out to flank James on either side.

James' route for escape lay behind him but he doubted that he could turn his horse quickly enough to avoid being hauled off his mount by the two burly soldiers to the side of him so he decided to employ a different tactic.

"Drink? I don't want to drink with you Thomayne but I would relish an opportunity to fight you, man to man, one on one, that is of course if you have the heart for it."

"The heart for a fight has never been in doubt in any of my opponents but my head says that you will be of more use to me as a prisoner. I am sure you have a lot of information that could help me in my quest to find Sargo."

"Sargo is gone to you Thomayne, stripped of her powers by the only living dragon in the world. There will be no more enemies dealt with by her for you, there will be no more magic bestowed to help you in your evil deeds. In fact it is only a matter of time before you come to realise that you have been a pawn in Sargo's quest to gain ultimate power over the country and that you, like everybody else that gets in her way, will be ultimately discarded like a tree discards its leaves. You will never find Sargo and if you think I would disclose her location, even if I knew where it was, you would be mistaken. So fight me Thomayne. Are you man enough or are you going to hide like a coward behind your soldiers?"

Thomayne's lips thinned as he drew them tighter in silent anger. He managed to remain composed though before he chose to speak.

"Is it a fight to the death you wish or a fight to secure your freedom against my desire for information?"

"Either suits me." James blurted out angrily before realising the implications of what he was saying.

"In that case we will fight for a prize as in a tournament. You win I will let you go a free man but if I win then you will tell me everything I wish to know agreed."

"Agreed."

"Right, then we will eat and drink before the fight like all civilised men should do and see if there is another way that we might both achieve our goals. Dismount and sit here!" He instructed.

The surprise of the invitation held James back for a few seconds too long and when he made no move to follow his instructions Thomayne nodded to the two men flanking James and each drew their swords and placed them at James's stomach. James dismounted and did as he was requested to do.

He sat next to Thomayne but when his men tried to relieve him of his sword James drew his dagger from his scabbard and held it to the man's chest.

"There is no need to relieve him of his sword, he is an honourable man, of that I am sure. Tend to the horses and leave us to talk." Thomayne barked at his man and James returned his dagger glad that his bluff had been enough to prevent him having to hurt another.

They ate in silence to begin with and James devoured enough meat to satiate his appetite without bloating himself which would reduce or impair his ability to fight. After that he shared some wine, which was not at all to his taste and waited for his captor to break the silence.

One of the guards removed his helmet and James recognised the bearded face of Sir Humphrey. Although he had moved away, like the other two, he hadn't gone so far and was within easy striking distance if James so much as stretched for his sword.

James remembered the skill with the sword that Humphrey had displayed at the tournament and nodded to the man when their eyes met in an unguarded moment.

"So Sir James, what is it in the entire world that you want the most? Is it titles, land, the hand of a fair maiden, tell me what it is so that I can grant you it and gain your loyalty."

"My loyalty is given freely to those I choose to give it to. Usually, it is bestowed to those who I have come to respect. I have no such feelings towards you for I have no idea who you really are.

You once sat at King Arthur's table as a trusted member of his knights but something happened to you. Either you were greedy and sought the help of Sargo to help you steal the sword and bring the country close to war or, you was selected by Sargo, without your knowledge and consent, to conduct yourself in the manner you have. It is clear to me that you, and many of the knights, and men that follow you, are still under the influence of her magic for you all fail to see the errors of your ways."

"Sargo worked for me and still will when I find her and return her to Castle Witch."

"If you ever found her, and I can tell you that you won't, all you would find is a pathetic old woman, who is well past the time of her demise and without any of the magic that she once commanded."

"You are bluffing of course Sir James for there is only one other that could possibly reduce her to the state that you have described. Merlin cannot fight the Witchcraft of Sargo in her own domain and that is why he has never come."

"There is another, but he cannot really be classed as a human, although he has more human qualities than you do at present. Surely you know who, what, can remove a Witches' powers don't you?"

"Again a good attempt to ruse me Sir James but everybody knows that the dragons have long since become extinct."

"All but one Sir Thomayne and he currently ally's himself to Merlin."

The sincerity of James words were getting through to Thomayne and he was growing impatient.

"Why do you persist with all this nonsense, none of what you have said is true and yet I have bestowed my generosity and sense of honour upon you this past hour. The time for talking is done Sir James and you and I will fight but the rules have just been changed. For dishonouring my generosity we will now fight to the death."

James felt a chill run through him as he realised the significance of what was about to happen. He hadn't seen Thomayne fight but he had to be good; he was a former member of the Knights of the Round Table after all. He put his fear away and stood up. He paced a few steps away from Thomayne before turning back and drawing his sword.

"Are you sure you want to do this?" He asked but there was no backing down from Thomayne and he drew his sword.

Then like the dance of strutting peacocks they slowly circled each other searching for any sign of weakness before Thomayne pounced swinging his sword high and bringing it down towards James' head. The force behind it jarred James' body as he raised his own to thwart the downward stroke but he held it and prevented it travelling further.

Thomayne withdrew it and circled some more. James looked him straight in the eye and watched for the slightest tell in them that would betray Thomayne's next attack. It came fast and there was no warning. This time he swung it from out wide aiming down to take out a leg, James' leg. James saw it coming and reacted just in time. He moved in the same direction as the incoming sword so that when he met it with his own the force had already been spent and he deflected it easily. Thomayne however, lost his balance as the momentum of his swing carried him further than he expected. With his guard temporarily down James could have run him through there and then but he didn't want to hurt this man so instead he waited for Thomayne to straighten and began the dance again.

"You could have finished me Sir James and that is a mistake that you will live to regret for I will not afford you such luxury when my turn comes, and it will come."

James said nothing and kept his eyes glued to his opponents. This time Thomayne came forward for a close quarter encounter with his sword and the two traded blow after blow with a skill level on a par with each other. James knew that there would be little quarter given in any exchange like this so he withdrew a few paces and circled some more.

The other three of Thomayne's men stood together now, a few yards away watching the two sword fighters with interest especially as they could see how even the contest looked. Suddenly, two of them left the ground as some unseen force hit them from behind. They landed just to the side of Thomayne who looked in bemusement at the carnage. Neither moved and were desperately fighting to regain their breath.

Sir Humphrey, the only one of the three still standing, was as equally surprised as Thomayne and was slow to react when a recognisable figure stood and pointed a sword directly at his chest. James moved in quickly and placed his sword tip at Thomayne's chest.

"Perhaps you would be good enough to sit for a moment Thomayne." He instructed and removed Thomayne's sword from his hand.

"You took your time Sir Matthew, what kept you," he asked his friend grinning.

"Sorry for the delay Sir James but I had to come, didn't want you to have all the fun now did I?" Matt returned with a grin as big as James.

"What shall we do with them?" James asked.

"Let's leave them here minus their horses whilst we ride for Camelot."

"Sounds like a good plan."

Matt slapped the horse's rumps and they sped off into the distance whilst James kept his sword firmly against Thomayne. Then he mounted his own ride and walked slowly towards James. Taking his own sword, he placed it alongside James' releasing him from the burden of guarding him. He walked to and mounted his horse before moving alongside Matt.

"I am extending you a courtesy; in return of the one you gave me earlier Sir Thomayne, by not tying you and your friends up. It is my hope that sometime in the near future you will be released from Sargo's magic and be able to return to your former life free to make your own decisions."

"If we ever meet again Sir James there will be no repetition of the courtesy I endowed upon you and I will run you through with my sword."

"It saddens me that you feel like that but I seriously doubt I will grace your company again. You might spare a thought or two about what you will say to King Arthur when we tell him of your involvement in everything."

Matt and James turned their mounts and started to canter away.

"I will kill you, you swine's, kill you do you hear me?" Thomayne shouted after them.

"Oh dear such bad manners James, I think he just called us pigs."

"Terrible Matt, though we have both heard worse on the rugby pitch."

The boys grinned at each other and then laughed as they rode west toward Camelot.

Chapter 20:
King Arthur

Matt and James rode silently for a while before Matt asked the question that had been on his mind for a while.

"Why didn't you call for Aragon's help when you fought Thomayne James? There was absolutely no need to risk injury or your life."

"It was a matter of honour really I suppose. Somewhere trapped and deep inside Thomayne is an honourable man and I hoped to remind him what it meant to be honourable. It probably didn't but it doesn't matter because I feel better for trying. I just hope that when the magic is removed from him, and the truth comes out, it was Sargo, who coerced him, rather than Thomayne who dreamed up the plot to get rid of Arthur."

"We should check in with Aragon to ensure that everybody is all right."

Matt made contact and was pleased to hear that the soldiers had left the wood immediately after James and Matt had. Their distraction had worked and Merlin, William and Mary were following the route west that Matt and James had selected but were at least ten miles distant behind them.

The potion that Merlin had given them to ward off their feelings of tiredness was weakening and both the boys were feeling tired. It was now two days and nights since they had last slept and Matt relayed that to Aragon.

Within minutes the sound of huge beating wings made them look upward to see Aragon above them. In his claw he held a small cloth bag held closed by a drawstring of twine. The dragon released it and James caught it.

"It is more of what you took before and it should be sufficient to last beyond reaching Camelot," Aragon told them.

Then with a few powerful beats the dragon soared away back in the direction it came from to continue his watchful vigil over Merlin.

After a further two hours Matt noticed a dust cloud in the distance to their left and they stopped to watch it. The cloud seemed to be approaching them and was increasing rapidly in size. A second cloud appeared to the right of them which followed the same developing pattern.

"What do you think it is James?" Matt asked.

"It reminds me of the sight of a combine harvester at harvest time. They always kick up a dust storm like that but they don't have combine harvesters during this time period. It has to be animals, a herd of animals like you see sometimes in an old cowboy movie when they take a herd of cows on the trail."

"I'll wager money that that is not being caused by cows, more like horses. I think we are about to be intercepted by an army. Could it be King Arthur's army?"

"It could be and by the speed they are travelling at they will be with us in a matter of minutes."

"What if it's not?"

"Nothing that we can do about this, we are either going to make new friends or more enemies."

The encroaching army closed in on them very quickly and individual horse and riders could be clearly made out at the front. The rear was completely swamped by the dust cloud though. The army came at them from both sides and met as they passed them completely circling them and cutting off any thought of escape.

"There are thousands of them Matt." James exclaimed the obvious.

The army came to a stop with the closest riders still ten yards or so away from them. Nobody moved any closer and the dust started to settle. The full extent of the army could be seen stretching into the distance all around them for as far as they could see.

Then some of the mounted soldiers separated slightly allowing a small gap to appear within their ranks and three heavily armoured riders approached them. They could see that their armour was of a finer quality than the majority of the soldiers around them and they guessed correctly as to who they were.

"The one in the centre James; that has to be King Arthur; look at the finery of decoration on his armour."

"Identify yourselves," the rider on the right called out.

"Sir Mathew and Sir James my lord," Matt responded.

"What business do you have on the King's Road?"

"Who do I have the honour of talking to my Lord?" James interrupted.

"Do you not recognise your King when you see him?" The knight on the right asked.

"My apologies sire, I have never had the fortune to be close enough to you to see your face clearly," James said bowing slightly to the King.

"We have ridden from Castle Witch with news for King Arthur about forces who plot against him; about the whereabouts of Excalibur, about the defeat of Sargo the Witch at Merlin's hand and about the plight of Merlin himself." Matt added quickly.

"Such matters are the reasons for our travel, it would appear that you are the two we seek."

"How can that be so since you could not have known of our presence here?"

"Dismount Sir Knights and take refreshment with your King and we will discuss these matters."

The King barked out some orders to his men and three blankets were laid on the ground. Then, as if a kitchen was only feet away, food appeared on plates and was placed on the centre blanket. Arthur dismounted and sat on one of the blankets and indicated for Matt and James to take the other. As they sat Arthur indicated to his men and they backed away allowing them to talk without being overheard.

Matt noticed that the King's sword scabbard was empty and untied his belt. Then he lay his own weapons to one side before sitting where the King had indicated. James followed his example.

"You grace me with your presence and your manners Sir Matthew perhaps you could enlighten me as to how this all got started for you and the part that you have played in it for I am astute enough to know that dark forces have prevailed over the region run by Castle Witch and your survival must be due to your skill and endeavours as well as with the help of my old friend Merlin."

With that said he removed the helmet from his head and Matt and James looked at the man of legends. Long dark and curly hair fell from his head and rested just below the shoulders. A broad chin and high forehead gave him an air of indestructibility whilst a delicate mouth and nose softened the features making him handsome in the eyes of most women. Then piercing blue eyes that hinted at the intelligence he carried, completed the features of the remarkable man.

Matt and James told him everything from the point that they had met Merlin even the fact that they were not really knights at all. Arthur listened with interest and amusement at some of the antics they had been up to. When they had finished The King announced his plans.

"Our first task is to find Merlin and have him prepare the magic that will return Thomayne and his men back to the characters they were before Sargo's magic changed them. Your friend Richard will also receive the magic, rest assured. Then it will be on to Castle Witch to seek out all those afflicted by the Witches curse and retrieve the sword that is rightfully mine and restore peace to this land.

"Despite the magnitude of all of this it is all merely a day's work in the life of a king. At some point during this excursion I would like to meet the dragon you call Aragon, he could be an ally in maintaining peace and order throughout my lands.

"William and Mary will be rewarded for their efforts, Richard too. It is good to know that I have loyal servants. But first there is one other task I have to perform.

Matt and James looked at him quizzically but the King said nothing but stood up.

"Please do me the courtesy of kneeling before me so that I can reward you in front of all my forces. Sir Henry, your sword please."

Sir Henry moved forward and drew his sword before handing it to Arthur.

In a loud and commanding voice the King began his rhetoric. "My lords I wish you to recognise the deeds that these men have performed on behalf of their King and country and witness the reward that I bestow upon them which seems barely enough to compensate them for their endeavours. By the King's command and in front of the witnesses present I grant you both the position of knight of the realm. He placed his sword on James' shoulder. "Arise Sir James." Then he placed it on Matt's shoulder and said, "Arise Sir Matthew.

"You are both welcome at the round table of Camelot whenever you are present. Land and Titles will be afforded to you at a more convenient time."

"Thank you Sire." Matt and James replied in harmony.

"There is one more request I have of you."

"Name it Sire."

"Will you both ride alongside me to Castle Witch?"

They mounted their horses and took their place alongside the King and received the calls of 'welcome brother knight' from those around them.

"Sire, you never answered my question," Matt pointed out.

"Which question was that?"

"How did you know where we were before you found us?"

"The strangest thing happened last night. There was a voice in my sleep, a dream but not a dream, I was awake but not awake. The voice told me to take my army and ride until I met Sir Matthew and Sir James. I was told to listen to your tale and act upon it. Oh yes, and you were supposed to give me something so that I would know that you came from Merlin."

He looked from one to the other.

James raised his hands to the back of his neck and untied the twine that secured the canine tooth. He passed it over to the King who smiled and placed it in a small bag on his saddle.

"I think it is time that the King should take the lead of his army. Protocol always dictates that the King rides some way back from the head of the army but to be honest I like riding at the front. Besides it ensures that we don't get covered in all that infernal dust."

He headed to the front and led his troops at a gentler pace this time than the one that he had set when he pursued Matt and James. They told him that it shouldn't be long before they met up with Merlin or Thomayne if he hadn't been rescued by his own forces. For an instant the sun was masked by something flying between it and them. James looked up and pointed to a dark shape high above them.

"If you look above you Sire you can see Aragon and I am sure that if you concentrate hard and focus on him you might be able to communicate with him."

"Do you think so?"

"I have just spoken to him and he says that it is only right that the King of the land should be able to speak to the last of the dragons. He wants to speak to you sire."

Chapter 21: Magical Moments

Two hours later, and while King Arthur was still reliving the fact that he had spoken to a real live dragon with amazement, they approached the wood where James and Matt had left Merlin, William and Mary.

Whilst Arthur and his army waited, Matt and James rode in to see if their friends were still there but to no avail. They expressed their concerns to Arthur when they returned.

"It is our fear that Thomayne has captured them for they are not where we left them and we haven't passed them on route," James told the King.

"A thought occurs to me that we have been doing this all wrong. It would be a much simpler task to ask Aragon the dragon who sees all. He would undoubtedly know where Merlin is," The King replied.

James was in communication with Aragon before the King had finished speaking.

"Good news, they have not been captured but were forced to detour when they spotted Thomayne and three others wandering their way. It would seem that the army returned to Castle Witch when their leader failed to return. Thomayne is several miles east of here with Merlin and the others somewhere in between. Aragon suggests they are just about to alter their course and travel west again."

"Let's not waste a minute then Sir James we need to get to Merlin as soon as possible."

They found Merlin less than ten minutes later and the King moved quickly towards him.

"It would seem old friend that I have dishonoured you whilst you have done nothing but honour me in the service of your King. Can you ever forgive me?"

"There is nothing to forgive my King, Sargo's powerful influence over mortal men cannot be underestimated and even a King may fall foul to it."

"You are more than generous, graceful too Merlin. I am fortunate to have one such as you to call my friend."

Merlin introduced William and Mary to the King and told them of the part they had played so far. Arthur listened carefully despite the fact that he had already heard about their exploits from Matt and James.

"I know that the Queen requires a new hand maiden Mary and that job could be yours if you want it and my lands need farmers of the quality of you William especially when they display such loyalty to the crown."

"Thank you sire we are both honoured and overwhelmed by your generous offers."

Arthur told Merlin to start preparing the magic so that he could free the afflicted from Sargo's hold. The army stayed where they were for the largest part of the afternoon before Merlin announced that he had everything he needed to begin blending the concoction.

Once he had done this the liquid was sieved through a piece of cloth and the remnants left behind were a picture of disgust to all those who witnessed it. Merlin discarded the waste and shook the water carrier that held the fluid.

"This will be ready when it goes completely clear. It will be odourless but once consumed it will not be without pain as the evil is driven from their bodies."

"Will it endure the constant jostling of travel?" The King asked and Merlin nodded.

"And will you ride by my side as you did when I first won my crown Merlin."

"It would be my Honour Sire."

"Then it is time that we catch up with Sir Thomayne and Sir Humphrey and friends."

They mounted their horses once more and Merlin took his place alongside Arthur whilst Matt slipped in alongside James just behind.

Thomayne and the three others were overrun by Arthur's army in less than half an hour. The four of them took up the defensive stature of back to back and showed no fear at the odds they were facing.

"Our meeting has arrived sooner than I expected but that is of no real concern. I would ask since your numbers are overwhelming that you show me the courtesy of meeting me in combat so that I might defeat you and take my rightful place on the throne."

"Your bravery has never been in doubt Sir Thomayne but it has been inflated exponentially by the Witchcraft of Sargo. You cannot, of course, be held responsible for your actions because of this but I am aware that you are completely ignorant to the fact and believe that you control Sargo."

He turned to Merlin. "Could you create an image of Sargo in her current state so that Sir Thomayne can behold what she has become?"

Merlin nodded and untied a wooden bowl that hung from his saddle. He dismounted and filled the bowl with water and proceeded to chant. Then he placed a stone in the centre and when the ripples that he had caused ceased an image formed. Sargo. Thomayne looked at it and spat in disgust at the image.

"There is only one thing that could reduce a great Witch to that condition and we all know that they don't exist."

"We tried to tell you before Thomayne that there is such a beast in existence but you chose not to believe us. So look for yourself." James said suddenly and a dark shadow which blotted out the sun appeared above them.

Slowly, it lowered until it landed deftly on the ground in front of Thomayne. He gasped in surprise before accusing them of magical trickery. Aragon snorted fire close enough to Thomayne to make him uncomfortably hot. He reeled back in surprise and looked at the burnt patch of grass close to his feet. He drew his sword but James slipped off his horse and stood between Aragon and Thomayne.

"I am aware that you want to defend yourself against Aragon and would like nothing else but to continue our personal fight but it just isn't the right time. Besides, despite what has happened to you I know there is still honour within you. As you did with me, I would like to return the courtesy of sharing a meal with you and if at the end of it you still wish to fight me then so be it."

The King lifted his eyebrows in surprise at James' offer to Thomayne but James gave him a look back that invited him to go along with whatever he was planning.

James called for blankets and food and set them down as Thomayne had done for him. Then some of the soldiers brought them food. He invited the other three members of Thomayne's group to join them and they tucked into some fresh meat. Next he asked Matt to fetch some water from Merlin's horse and Matt immediately grasped what James had planned and poured four containers with the now clear potion that Merlin had prepared.

James' guests drank greedily and talked avidly as if they didn't have a care in the world despite being surrounded by thousands of soldiers.

"Sir Thomayne, in a moment I am told that you will experience some pain, as will your three friends. It will be uncomfortable for a while but it offers freedom from the shackles of Sargo's magic. Let this pass through and purge your body for on completion you will be as you once were."

"What deception is this?" Thomayne cried out but a spasm of pain caused him to double over in reflex. The same pain gripped his friends and none of them could prevent themselves from crying out with the force of it.

For thirty long minutes the pain continued until a black cloud started to pour from each man's mouth and raise slowly skyward. Aragon flared his nostrils and sent a flame that incinerated the black cloud completely and the evil had gone. The men stopped groaning and looked up to see their King.

"Sire, where am I, how did I get here?" Thomayne asked in genuine surprise.

"Do not concern yourself with such matters right now Sir Thomayne. It is good to have you back; will you ride with me as you did at the battle of Sessingford?"

It would honour me sire." Thomayne answered proudly.

They mounted once more and this time there were no more stops to make before they reached Castle Witch.

Darkness had moved in to mask their arrival at the castle and every other soldier carried a torch. Arthur wanted those at the castle to see the strength of the force that lay siege to them in an effort to prevent bloodshed. The ploy worked and they were allowed entry into the castle where every man was rounded up and moved to the dungeons whilst the castle was searched for those who did not want to reveal themselves.

When he was satisfied that all were in his power Arthur ordered the potion to be given to every man, woman and child. He could not afford to take the chance to overlook the possibility that even the smallest child might be compromised by the Witch's magic.

They worked systematically through each dungeon freeing everyone after the magic had been expelled from their bodies and incinerated by Aragon.

William searched for his cousin and watched as he endured the pain and then witnessed the magic leave his body. He embraced him as he was released and took him to where James and Matt waited. Strangely, those who had not been cursed by the Witch did not suffer any discomfort from the potion.

When the last of the dungeon occupants were freed Merlin approached the King and told him that there was just one more task to perform. At first the King didn't seem to understand, still caught up with the melee of everything that had happened, but then his hand clutched involuntarily at the empty scabbard at his side as he realised he still hadn't reclaimed ownership of his sword.

"Perhaps Merlin, Sir James, Sir Matthew and William should be the ones that show me where the sword is located since they were the ones who carried at great odds with Sargo's magic. Mary too, I hear that it was her who helped them with the last few feet." He said smiling.

James indicated to William for him to lead the way and the man's chest expanded with pride.

"Follow me Sire if you please," He said and led the way from the dungeons to the stable area.

Mary filled in the details for the King on how she had followed the man that took Excalibur to its temporary home. He listened intently and praising her for her bravery.

"It's just through this door Sire," William told the King as they approached the stables.

"What door, I can see no door?" The King replied.

"This door Sire!" William said and lifted the concealed latch. He pushed it open and Arthur could see inside.

"I take it that this is your magic Merlin and not Sargo's."

Merlin smiled his grimace and nodded.

When they were all inside William waited for Merlin to remove the magic that concealed the sword and then pushed away the straw that still covered it.

There on the earth lay Excalibur.

"Would you pick it up for me Sir James?" The King asked.

James bent down and tried to lift the sword.

"I am afraid I cannot move it Sire"

"Sir Matthew?"

Matt tried but he already knew that he would not be able to move it.

"And what about you Merlin, can you move it with your magic?"

"If I could have I would not have left it here my Lord. Not even my magic can help me lift it. That is for you alone."

King Arthur smiled bent down and effortlessly picked up Excalibur. He looked at it as warmly as if he was greeting an old friend before placing it in his scabbard.

"I have rewarded everyone who has helped me in this adventure except two. Merlin you will take your place at Camelot when we return and help me rule this country of ours and maintain the peace. But then there is Aragon. What is it that I can give a dragon as a measure of my gratitude?"

"That is easy my Lord," a voice in his head answered.

"All I desire is to be able to live in peace and not be hunted as my ancestors were. In return for this I will promise my assistance in any matter that you need me for."

"Now that is a deal worthwhile making Aragon and I shall make it known to all that it is my desire to free you from any persecution."

"Thank you my King."

Chapter 22: The Return

The group started to make their way back towards the castle when William, who led the way, stopped suddenly and started to rub his forehead. He turned and held up his hand just in time to stop Matt and James from experiencing what he just had.

"What is it William, why have you stopped?" Matt asked in surprise.

"A barrier, an invisible barrier. It wasn't here when we passed this way to get to the sword but now it is and it stops us returning inside the castle."

Matt and James both extended their arms and touched the barrier. It didn't feel like anything they had touched before, in fact it seemed to have no real substance, not hard or soft, not warm or cold. It was there though and the two of them worked their way along it in opposite directions.

"I can't find an end to it!" Matt exclaimed.

"Me neither!" James added.

"What is going on Merlin?" Arthur demanded.

"It is magic, of that I am certain. I will try to counteract it," the magician answered, surprise evident in his voice.

He started to chant in the same strange language that Matt and James had heard before. On and on he went but nothing happened and the barrier remained in place.

"It is strong magic, too strong." Merlin stated.

"If you can't remove it can you puncture it so that we may pass through?" James asked.

Merlin tried again but with the same result.

"Who could have done this Merlin and why," The King demanded.

"I am not sure Sire. With Sargo already dealt with it is not clear. There are several other Witches with the power but I cannot imagine their motivation."

"Their motivation is not important for the moment, what is important is that all the people who were here at Castle Witch during Sargo's reign know that I am in control, not another Witch, and at the moment it seems that I am not," the King stated.

"Aragon, see if this barrier spreads all the way around the castle."

The dragon disappeared and then returned after a few minutes his voice appearing inside the heads of Matt, James, Merlin and the King.

"The barrier stretches all around the castle except the seaward side. The cliffs are barrier enough."

"It would appear that we cannot get into the castle then. Merlin's magic is not strong enough to penetrate the barrier and there is no other way in," the King said with real frustration.

"There is a way Sire, I know how we can get into the castle," Matt said suddenly.

Everybody turned towards him expectantly.

"The dungeons that's where we can get in."

"The cliffs are far too dangerous to climb Sir Matthew," Merlin stated.

"Not climb, fly! Aragon can fly us into one of the dungeons, all we need is one with an unlocked door."

"You can do this Aragon?" Merlin asked.

"It would not be difficult and not take too long, in fact it would probably take longer to find a dungeon with an open door."

"Should we not plan what to do when we get inside the castle?" The King asked.

"It is difficult to plan for the unknown. At the moment all we know is that we have been kept out of the castle by a barrier that has been placed by a Witch. We need to get in and find her," Merlin answered.

"The people inside may have been changed by magic like Sargo did before."

"Sargo was the strongest Witch I have ever encountered, I know of no other that would have the power to create the barrier and hold control over all the castle inhabitants."

"Why don't Matt and I go first to find an open dungeon and the rest of you can join us when we have?" James suggested.

"Merlin and I will be the only ones to join you." A small party holds a greater chance of going undiscovered. Besides William and Mary have done enough for their King already," Arthur stated.

William was about to say something but Matt held his hand up and said that the King was right

Aragon landed a few feet behind them and invited Matt and James to climb aboard. They sat between some of the ridges on his spine and held on to ridge in front. Aragon lifted effortlessly and the two boys found themselves flying around the castle.

"This is so cool James," Matt said with the excitement coursing through every ounce of his body.

"Do not get used to this for it will not happen a second time." Aragon told them.

At the back of the castle Aragon descended down towards the sea and rose up against the cliff face. He hovered at the mouth of a dungeon and James jumped off to check the door.

Between them Matt and James checked seven before they found one open. Aragon left them there while he returned to fetch the King and Merlin. They arrived soon and thanked Aragon for his assistance before he left them there.

Matt led the way along the narrow tunnel before heading up the stone steps that led to the abandoned hall. They passed through unseen and Merlin stopped.

"What is it old friend?" The King asked.

"I can feel the magic emanating from in there somewhere, he said pointing toward the direction of the banqueting hall that Matt and James had used when they were a guest of Thomayne's.

They were startled as a couple of soldiers appeared suddenly and came towards them.

The King gripped Excalibur's handle, ready to draw it, but the soldiers dipped their heads as they passed by and disappeared into the gloom of the night.

"It would appear that you were correct Merlin, those two showed no sign of being possessed by magic," the King said with an element of relief.

"It may be that we have only the Witch herself to deal with then Sire," the old man replied wearily.

They headed to the hall and found the door slightly open. It wasn't much but it was sufficient for them to see in without being noticed themselves.

James looked in and reeled back suddenly in shock at what he had seen. He led the others away from the hall before speaking.

"It's Sargo, she's different somehow, younger than when we left her but older than she was before. It's definitely her."

"It is as I feared. Aragon's power was insufficient against the great power that Sargo had amassed. He succeeded in draining some of her magic force but not all. Some has returned and it is only a question of time before she is able to return to her former position of power. She needs to be stopped now!" Merlin stated.

"How long do we have Merlin?" Matt asked.

"With the passing of each hour she grows stronger. The barrier she has placed on the castle is stretching her abilities for the moment and will contribute to slowing her down. Now it is the right time to act before she gets too strong."

"But what can we do?"

"We need her in the open again for Aragon to embrace her with dragon fire."

"It didn't completely work last time Merlin what makes you think it will work this time?"

"A second dousing of dragon fire will destroy her forever Sir Matthew. It is drastic I know but there is no other choice."

"How can we get her outside if she doesn't want to go?"

"I will use my power. It should be stronger than hers."

"You will have a few hours to hold her Merlin before midnight, can you do it?"

"I think so?"

Chapter 23:
Magic War

Merlin led the way back to the entrance of the great hall and pushed open the door. It swung open silently and the group entered.

Sargo had her back towards them and stood close to and facing an open fire. The flames curled round the huge logs that it was consuming and flickered in random triumph as it sent flames high into the chimney.

They approached to within a few metres of her before she turned. A smile broke on her face and she beamed it to each of her uninvited guests.

"So you managed to penetrate the barrier Merlin," she said with a deeper voice than they had heard before.

"And you managed to survive the dragon's fire," Merlin responded.

"Luck was with me for the dragon was underdeveloped."

"You know what happens if a dragon fires you for a second time?"

"I do but it will not happen."

"Your confidence is admirable but unfortunately misplaced Sargo."

"My confidence is not misplaced Merlin for even as we speak the King is no longer able to move."

They all turned to look at the King who had a look of surprise on his face. As they stared at him the look remained fixed as did his eyelids which no longer blinked.

"Release him at once Sargo," James ordered angrily.

"Or what?" Sargo said smiling with the same radiance that she had done before her encounter with Aragon.

James moved forward with surprising speed and Sargo wasn't expecting it. He reached out and circled her with his arms and locked his fingers. She screamed with a mixture of surprise and shock and started to wriggle, but James was more than a match for her physical strength.

He looked across to Matt as if to ask now what but the look went unnoticed as Merlin moved in front of him and started to chant. James felt a chill wash across his body and then found he couldn't move. He could hear everything that was said but couldn't respond in any way.

"What have you done Merlin?" Matt asked.

"I have placed on them a similar spell as Sargo placed on our King. They are locked together like this until I choose to remove the spell."

"When will that be? I don't like to see James stuck with that Witch."

"The spell only worked because Sir James was included. It was different than the one she used because of him. They will need to stay together until the hour approaches midnight when Aragon can finish the job he started. He lowered his voice so that only Matt could hear. I will release them at the very last moment. You will need to move fast and get Sir James away from her immediately for there will be only seconds in which to act."

"We can't get Aragon through the barrier which means that he won't be able to use his fire on Sargo."

"It is my thinking that Aragon could approach from above. The barrier probably doesn't extend beyond the height of the tallest tower."

"Get him to go now Merlin and wait in the jousting arena."

Merlin relayed the message to Aragon and then told Matt to go and get four soldiers. He returned a few minutes later with the men that Merlin had requested.

They bowed at the King and looked surprised when they received no response from him.

Merlin said a few unrecognisable words and the soldier's disposition changed.

"What is it that you need Merlin?" One asked.

"Follow my orders without question." Merlin started. "You two take the King and place him in the Royal Box at the jousting arena. See that he sits in a chair and is supported from falling."

Matt looked a little concerned about this and Merlin whispered that he had placed an obedience spell on the soldiers. He turned towards the other two soldiers.

"You two are to take Sir James and Sargo to the centre of the jousting arena. They are not to be prised apart and must be left standing exactly as they are now."

The soldiers nodded and moved towards James and Sargo.

Merlin tuned and left them to it.

"Come Sir Matthew there are things that we need to take care of."

"What things?"

"Things that could potentially save Sir James' life if all does not go to plan. Show me where the kitchen is for I have a spell to prepare."

Matt showed him the way and watched as a peculiar mix of ingredients were boiled in a pan and steeped for half an hour. Merlin told Matt that, like the potion he had made for Thomayne, the mixture needed to turn clear before it was ready for use.

"What exactly is it for Merlin?" Matt asked.

Sir James is to be covered in this before we separate him from Sargo.

"This will protect him from her?"

"No it will protect him from the fire of Aragon if you do not get him away from her in time. You will also need to be covered in this."

Half an hour before midnight Matt and Merlin went to the jousting arena. There in the centre, Sargo and James stood statuesque still locked together. The King sat in the royal box as motionless as James and Sargo and Aragon waited patiently to one side of the arena.

Matt and Merlin walked towards the dragon and greeted it warmly. Merlin told him the plan they had carefully crafted and Aragon voiced his concern for James and Matt's safety.

"If they are not coated completely with the potion they will die from my flames. It is not my wish to endanger those who have become friends."

"I understand the risk Aragon and I know that James would not hesitate to do for me what I am about to do for him."

"Do you not fear for your life Sir Matthew?"

"Trust me Aragon I want to live so of course there is fear, but fear can be healthy. It can heighten your senses and make you act faster and without thought."

"It can also make you reckless."

"Are you trying to make me feel better or worse?"

"I am making you aware."

"Consider it done Aragon."

"Come Sir Matthew, time is running short, help me apply the potion to Sir James but be careful not to get any on Sargo. I do not want even the smallest part of her protected."

They covered James as best as they could but where he gripped Sargo, parts of his arms and hands could not be covered. Matt expressed his concern but Merlin told him not to worry.

Merlin helped Matt cover himself with the potion and Matt was surprised that it dried almost immediately.

When the task was finished Merlin walked back towards Aragon and beckoned Matt to move to.

Quietly Merlin gave his instructions.

"When I release the spell on them they will move. Matt you are to make sure that James lets Sargo go and get him away from her as quick as possible. Aragon you are to flame her the second he is away. Even if Sir James is too close you must still use the flame. Sir Matthew can protect Sir James' hands and arms from your fire and literally walk out of it. She must not be allowed to leave the flames. Are you both clear on what you have to do?"

They confirmed their understanding and Aragon moved to the side of James and Sargo. Matt took position behind James so that Sargo wouldn't see him and guess his intention.

"There are just a few minutes to go Sir Matthew, Aragon; move when I say and move fast."

The remaining few minutes lasted an eternity for Matt as he waited to save his friend. Every muscle in his body was tensed ready for action.

"Now." Merlin shouted and released James and Sargo from his spell.

Matt launched into action forcing James' grip on Sargo apart before he had even realised he could move. Then Matt pulled him away but not before he found himself engulfed in flames. He kept pushing James away shielding his arms and hands with his own body. He burst out of the fire and turned to watch Sargo's fate. Still engulfed in the flames she had moved sideways in an effort to escape them and was just a few feet away from exiting the flames.

Matt watched in horrified silence. She was smoking from everywhere on her body, black thick smoke poured from her and her skin was turning black too. Still the Witch fought to get away and just when Matt thought she was too late she burst from the flames screaming a blood curdling scream that would have terrified the hardiest of men.

Merlin cried out in frustration and anger, James was still adapting to being out of the spell that had kept his body rigid for several hours and Aragon didn't seem to realise that Sargo had escaped his flames.

Matt took a deep breath and ran at Sargo. His momentum carried her back into the flames and Matt was unable to prevent himself from entering.

Sargo slipped and fell and Matt fell over her. He lay face down in the flames, quiet and still.

Sargo could not get up either and as Merlin and James watched with a morbid fascination her body turned to dust. Sargo was dead.

The flames ceased and Aragon's great head lowered. The creature had insufficient strength left to hold it up. He swayed a little, unsteady on his feet.

Merlin and James moved forward to where Matt lay and helped him up.

"Sir Matthew are you all right?" Merlin asked.

"Man that was intense. I'm fine Merlin, really."

"You were incredibly brave to go back into Aragon's fire."

"Or stupid!" James added.

"Couldn't let that Witch get away now could I?"

From out of the royal box the King came down to the arena.

"Sir Matthew, this country owes you a great debt. Even as I was locked into stillness I was able to see what you did. Your bravery is unrivalled."

"Thank you sire, but as a knight of the round table it should be."

"Let me escort you in and share a wine with you all," the King demanded.

"I must stay and tend to Aragon he is weakened from his efforts," Merlin told the King.

Arthur stroked the dragon's head and murmured his thanks before leaving with Matt and James. He called out to Merlin to join them when he could.

Chapter 24:
Home and Sleep

The King ordered a feast to celebrate the return of Excalibur and the end of the domination over the region by Sargo the Witch.

The festivities were already in full flow when James and Matt joined Merlin who sat a little way off from the King. Richard, William and Mary sat on a table next to the nobles as personal guests of King Arthur and whilst Matt and James had been invited to the same table they declined under the excuse that they were running some errands and would be late arriving. Of course there had been no such errands and the boys just wanted some time to collect their thoughts and plan what to do next.

"I think we have done all that we came here to do Matt."

"I think you're right, everything seems to have been sorted out and there is nothing left to do."

"Are you thinking what I am thinking then?"

"What, that it's time to leave here? I think so."

"If we wait a little while longer everyone here will start becoming a little worse for wear as they become drunk and we should be able to slip away unnoticed."

"Agreed, but we have a longer than normal journey back to the waterfall though."

"Yes, and I don't know about you but I am starting to feel the effects of not getting enough sleep in this place."

"Home and bed does sound like a great idea."

They continued in the merriment of the celebrations for another hour and watched Richard and William acting out parts of the adventure they had partook in, and Mary, already a favourite of the King, pouring wine for him.

Merlin sat quietly enjoying the spectacle too but refrained from joining in the banter, content enough to watch as Matt and James were. He excused himself a few moments before James decided that the time was right and the two of them left a moment later. They walked at a steady pace towards the portcullis and were just adjacent to the stables when the concealed stable door opened and Merlin appeared before them.

"I overheard your conversation that you were about to leave and thought to add my thanks to you for the assistance you gave me in earning favour back with my King."

"You don't need to thank us Merlin, we are friends are we not?"

"Indeed we are Sir Matthew. It occurred to me that I have taken you a long way from where I met you and that it is somewhere beyond there that you journey to. It is only fitting that two knights of the realm have mounts to speed them on their way. Remember always that you are Knights, follow the Knight's code, be good to those beneath you and honour all men. The King himself has endowed this upon you and as such you represent him in everything you say and do. Go with speed and with my gratitude."

Two magnificent, black stallions appeared from behind them and nudged them gently in the back as if encouraging them to leave.

"Thank you Merlin, they will shorten our journey considerably."

They mounted and took one last look at the magician of legend, turned the horses and moved away.

"Oh when the potion wears off that kept you awake for so long be warned that you will sleep for longer than usual." Merlin called.

"I think it's starting to wear off already," James called back.

The magic was wearing off for they scarcely noticed the length of the journey back to Merlin's shelter.

"Not too much further now Matt," James called out.

Then a voice appeared in both their heads.

"Did you really think you could leave without saying goodbye to the only living dragon in existence?"

"Aragon, is it really you?"

"Who else can communicate through the mind alone?"

"It is good to hear you one last time Aragon. I guess you have a lot of work ahead of you for I am sure that you and Merlin will be instrumental in helping the King maintain the peace."

"Alas a dragon's work is never done, there's scarcely time to finish growing."

"How big are you going to get?" Matt asked.

"Five times bigger than I am now."

"Wow! That's a lot of growing."

"Indeed! The waterfall you came through is not far from here and I assume that you will be unable to take the horses with you so if you leave them here I will return them to Merlin."

"How did you know that we came through the waterfall?" James asked surprised.

"I witnessed your appearance along the ledge. I have to say that I was surprised! I never guessed there was a cave behind it but it is an excellent place to conceal one self. I have heard your thoughts that tell of home when you pass through it. Tell me is it big enough to house me?"

"I'm afraid not Aragon, you won't fit in there especially if you are going to be as big as you say. There's room enough for a couple of humans and their belongings but that's it. Nobody else knows about the waterfall, except for one who lived long ago."

"Your secret is safe with me Sir Matthew and Sir James. Anyway, it is time for me to depart. Until things are completely back to normal I must stay near Merlin and ensure that he is safe."

"He is lucky to have a friend like you Aragon."

"As I am to have him; I would consider you as my friends too."

"Thank you and that goes both ways for us."

The voice in their heads disappeared and they dismounted and walked the rest of the way to the waterfall.

Approaching it James commented. "As much as I enjoy our adventures I am glad that the portal goes both ways and we can return home after each of them."

"Me too! Come on let's go, I need some sleep."

Matt passed through the deluge and James followed and they looked back at the torrent of falling water.

"Are you wondering where it will lead us next time Matt?"

"I sure am but it can wait a while I get some rest.

Then I'm coming back to make some more new friends in a different place and time."

"I'll be right there with you buddy."

'The Walking With Series'

by C. S. Clifford:

For the 8 – 13 age group:

Walking with the Hood

ISBN: 9780993195730

'The Walking With Series'

by C. S. Clifford:

For the 8 – 13 age group:

Walking with Nessie

ISBN: 9780993195709

'The Walking With Series'

by C. S. Clifford:

For the 8 – 13 age group:

Walking with the Fishermen

ISBN: 9780993195723

C. S. Clifford has always been passionate about stories and storytelling. As a child he earned money singing at weddings in the church choir; the proceeds of which were spent in the local bookshop.

He has taught in primary schools for the past ten years and was inspired to start writing through the constant requests of the children he teaches. He lives in Kent where, when not writing or teaching, he enjoys carpentry and both sea and freshwater angling.